ESCAPE FROM ZOMBIE CITY

(A ONE WAY OUT NOVEL)

THE ZOMBIE FEED PRESS

LEXINGTON, KY

This collection is a work of fiction. All the characters and events portrayed in these stories are either fictitious or are used fictitiously.

Escape from Zombie City

Cover design by Thomas A. Erb
Interior design by Ty Schwamberger & Sheryl Scanlon

Published by The Zombie Feed Press, an imprint of
Apex Publications, LLC
PO Box 24323
Lexington, KY 40524

www.thezombiefeed.biz
www.apexbookcompany.com

First Edition: October 2011

ISBN PB: 978-1-937009-01-4

Author's note:

A One Way Out novel, much like the Choose Your Own Adventure books I used to love reading back in elementary school, is not meant to be read straight through. At the end of each chapter, you will be presented with choices. Each of these choices will lead you along a different path through the book. There are many different endings, and as this is a horror story, the vast majority of the endings are rather... unpleasant. Only one path will get you through the story safely. Only one results in your survival. Best of luck finding the One Way Out. You're going to need it.

Ray Wallace

Of all the days to sleep in...

Ah, well, no point in worrying about things that can't be undone, you tell yourself. Spilled milk and all that.

You rolled out of bed about half an hour ago, just after eleven o'clock in the morning, and now here you stand on the tiny balcony of the outrageously priced one bedroom apartment you rent downtown near the heart of the city. Leaning out over the railing at the balcony's edge, you look straight down to the street six stories below. Traffic is usually pretty heavy in this part of town but today there really aren't that many cars. But there are plenty of people. Most of them are walking, at first glance give the appearance of friends out for a leisurely stroll. But there's something odd about the way they move, about the way they drift in small packs toward some of the other people who are moving a bit faster, some of these others running for all they are worth, obviously in an attempt to get away from the strangely organized packs that are following them. The sounds of shouting reach your ears. Someone is crying out for help. There is a high-pitched scream which cuts off abruptly.

You look to your left toward the four lane intersection there. As you watch, two cars slam into each other head-on. The noise from the impact causes your gut to churn. Steam pours up from beneath the hood of one of the cars. Some of the drifting packs of people make their way over to the scene of the accident. There is more screaming.

From somewhere in the distance there comes the rumbling sound of a large explosion followed by the tiny *pops!* of what can only be gunfire.

Directly across the street stands a building that is the mirror image of your own. A fifteen story apartment building with balconies just wide enough for maybe three people to stand comfortably side by side jutting outward into space. Two stories down you see a middle-aged woman back out through an open sliding glass door onto one of the balconies. She has her hands out in front of her in a defensive position. "No, no, no!" you hear her plainly exclaim. A man emerges from the interior of the apartment beyond, embraces the woman who has backed up against the railing and has nowhere further to go. She screams as the man leans in like he is going to give her a kiss but instead buries his face in her neck and starts to wrench his head back and forth like a dog going at a piece of meat. Her screaming is a terrible thing as she leans back far enough to topple up and over railing, pulling her attacker with her. You watch as the two of them plummet the approximately fifty feet to the street below.

"Welcome to the end of the world," you say, then turn around and head through the open sliding glass door behind you back into your apartment.

The TV is on, a nice, big screen flat panel that is mounted to one of the walls, the sound provided by a high-end surround system with speakers discreetly hidden in the corners of the room. One of the news channels is on and showing footage from a helicopter hovering over one of the city's half dozen parks.

"*It seems that the numbers of the undead are increasing rapidly, exponentially, surprising experts and law enforcement alike,*" a voice-over is narrating as the view zooms in toward one of the packs of the undead closing in on some sorry bastard who has apparently injured himself and is trying to crawl away as quickly as he can. But it's not nearly fast enough for he is soon overcome. The camera reverse zooms as the man is pulled limb from limb in a grisly tug-of-war between a number of the monsters that have taken hold of him.

The walking dead, you think. *Can this really be happening?* In the space of several hours the world you've known has become a horror show. From the fifteen minutes or so of TV you watched after getting out of bed, before heading out onto the balcony to see things firsthand, you know that a virus is being blamed. A *man-made* virus. Apparently, there was an explosion in one of the buildings over by the stadium early this morning, sometime before sunrise. Several people were killed in the blast. There are unconfirmed reports that the building housed a lab of some sort. A lab possibly owned by an as-yet-to-be named (or blamed) branch of the military. The explosion ripped a large hole in one of the building's walls. Ever since, a dark gas has been pouring forth from the opening, forming an ever larger cloud that has spread outward across that section of the city. Camera views from a news helicopter have shown the area enveloped in a thick, inky mist. A mist that sickens and quickly kills anyone who is unfortunate enough to inhale it. And then brings them back to life as the walking dead.

Now, how is that for a little Saturday morning entertainment?

Of all the days to sleep in, you chastise yourself once again. But how were you to know that today would be the day that the dead would walk? If this was the sort of information that you were privy to, then certainly you would not have gone out with the few people from work you actually consider friends of yours and thrown back as many beers as you had, now would you? Or maybe you would have imbibed a bit more heavily.

As you watch, the picture on the TV cuts to the interior of a news studio with a pair of suitably grim-faced reporters sitting behind a long desk. In the upper right hand corner of the screen there is a graphic depicting a biohazard symbol with the words "Zombie Emergency!" in bright red letters superimposed on top of it. The newscasters spend a couple of minutes discussing another as-yet-unconfirmed report, this one pertaining to a possible intermediate phase in the transition from healthy, living human being to full-fledged zombie.

"*We here at News Channel 10 have been inundated with eyewitness accounts of extremely violent individuals randomly attacking people throughout the city. These individuals are said to scream incoherently, earning them the name 'howlers'. They seem completely oblivious to any physical harm they may suffer. It is said that these howlers will eventually tire and collapse to the ground. Then they will rise as the living dead... We must reiterate that these accounts are unconfirmed. Neither law enforcement officials nor members of the scientific community have weighed in on this story. If you do happen to encounter someone displaying this sort of irrational behavior, it is suggested that you vacate the area as quickly and safely as possible.*"

The picture switches to a close-up of one of the reporters, an attractive, middle-aged woman with shoulder length brown hair. "*In other, related news... Within the hour, the mayor is expected to take to the airwaves and address the present, still unfolding situation. Exactly what actions are being taken to achieve some semblance of order are–"*

And that's when the power goes dead.

"Great," you mutter. As if a zombie apocalypse isn't bad enough. Now there's the very real possibility you may have to face it without any AC. Or television. Or a working refrigerator. And all that beer in there...

The idea of being eaten by a pack of zombies doesn't seem all that bad at the moment.

That's just the shock talking, you tell yourself. For, undoubtedly, you really haven't been yourself since rolling out of bed and switching on the TV. And who can blame you? Life had been moving along in a sure and steady routine until the dead decided they didn't want to stay dead anymore. You were due a promotion at work. More money. More vacation time. Fall is finally settling in and the sweltering summer heat has started to abate. A little bit, at least. The holidays are fast approaching and you've been looking forward to hopping on an airplane and getting together with friends and family members you haven't seen in a while. And now this...

There is the sound of another explosion from somewhere outside.

Yeah, a terrible day to sleep in. Should have gotten out of town hours ago...

You look at your cell phone where you left it lying on the couch the night before. Picking it up, you try to make a call, selecting a random friend's number, find that the network is overwhelmed, that all you get is a recorded message asking you to please try again later...

So now here you are, cut off from everyone you know, still a relative newcomer to the city, the metaphorical stranger in a strange land, the recipient of a company transfer that brought you here only a few short months ago. You've been working so much that you really haven't had any time to make new friends. Sure, there are the few from work you've had drinks with but it's not like you've been planning on exchanging Christmas presents or heading off for a weekend getaway with any of them any time soon. That level of friendship has not been established, maybe never will, especially in light of today's events. It's dawning on you that you're going to have to face the nightmare taking over the world around you on your own. If you're going to try to make your way out of the city, you're going to have to do so by yourself. Undoubtedly, the idea of going out there, of leaving the apartment, is more than a bit overwhelming. Maybe if you just stay put, ride things out for a while... There are plenty of canned goods in the kitchen cabinets. Bottles of water. Cold beer. Well, cold for a few hours at least. And the power is sure to come back on at some point...

There's a knock at the door. More like a pounding, actually, like someone is using an open hand, slapping at the door. The sound comes again, slow and deliberate. You circle the couch and make your way over to the door, lower your eye to the peephole. What you see through that tiny window causes a chill to go down your spine and a tightness to form in your gut. His face...Well, it's a bit of a mess. One of the eyes is missing, a dark, gaping socket where it used to be. Most of the flesh on that side of the face has been torn away all the way down to the jawline. You can see the teeth there, the man's molars pressed tightly together. The eye that's still intact stares back at you through the peephole, unblinking. The flesh along the chin, above the upper lip, and covering the cheek that is still intact sports a five o'clock shadow. The dead man slaps at the door again causing you to jump back from the door. Now you can hear the sound of the zombie moaning.

So here it is, the terrible thing that is happening to the city brought to your front door. The way you see it, you can fight, you can run, or you can hide. But a decision has to be made. Whatever the decision, though, there is something you must do first to ensure your chances of survival.

You walk at a brisk pace through the living area then down the short hallway to the apartment's lone bedroom. Inside, there is a bed, of course, a nightstand, a dresser, a closet door, and a wooden chest on the floor at the foot of the bed. You drop to your knees on the carpeting before the chest and open it. Inside there is a metal lockbox filled with various odds and ends including spare keys to your apartment and your car, a passport, and some extra check books. Next to the metal box is a small cardboard box and a black plastic case, both of which you lift from the chest. You close the chest, set the case and the small box on top of it, then pop open the pair of clasps which hold shut the case. From within, you remove the loaded, snub nosed, .38 caliber handgun. The small cardboard box is filled with spare cartridges. You put the box in the front pocket of the jeans you are wearing. The gun feels good in your hand. You've fired it plenty of times at a local indoor range but have never had to use it on a person, alive or undead. Shortly after moving to the city, a colleague at work had suggested you purchase the gun.

"There's no shortage of criminals in this city," he'd told you, suggesting the weapon might come in handy if there was a break-in. You've never really been convinced of this but now you're glad you took the advice and purchased the weapon. The thing could definitely come in handy now. There is a zombie outside your front door. Somehow, by either stumbling into the elevator or wandering up the stairs, it has made it up to your floor. And where there is one, there could be more, may already be more on the way. Three courses of action, you tell yourself once again. Fight, flight, or do nothing. An amalgam of emotions swirls through you as you try to decide what to do. There is fear, of course, as this very surreal situation now poses a tangible threat. There is also anger at what the undead have done to your world, at the fact that they have caused you to be afraid like this. And there is a deep sense of frustration as you stand there, momentarily frozen in the grip of uncertainty, unsure of what you should do.

If you give in to your anger and decide to fight, turn to page 8.

If you allow your fear to control you, turn to page 10.

If the battling emotions leave you incapable of making a decision, turn to page 12.

You may not be the bravest individual alive, but this... This is too much. And it simply cannot be abided. A zombie. Standing at your door. Slapping its hand against it. As if it was demanding entry. Like this was *its* apartment or something. Like maybe *you* are the intruder here. Or maybe you had wronged the undead thing somehow. The nerve.

Without pausing to think about what you are doing—because then the fear might get its claws into you—you march back out to the front door, unlock it, grab the handle, give it a turn and pull the door open. And there it is, the zombie, standing a few feet in front of you, hand raised as if in the act of waving hello. The smell of the thing hits you, a thick, sweet odor of decay and uncontrolled bodily functions. Bile rises in your throat as you lift the gun, aim it straight at the zombie's heart, and pull the trigger. At this range, the sacrifice in accuracy the snub nose design burdens its shooter with is not an issue. The report of the gun is loud in the enclosed space. The weapon bucks in your hand as it releases its power. The undead thing before you stumbles backward as if someone has come up behind it and pulled it off balance. It backs into the door across the hall where its backpedaling is halted. You can see the hole in the cloth of the dirty, white button down shirt that the zombie is wearing, the kind of shirt that a banker or an insurance salesman might wear. When the sound of the shot dissipates you can hear the zombie moaning. It is still on its feet and now it is pushing away from the wall, raising both hands and taking a step toward you.

Without thinking about it, you raise the gun and take aim at the center of the zombie's forehead. Perfect kill shot just like you've practiced on the targets at the range. Another squeeze of the trigger, another loud report, and this time the zombie's legs buckle as its head snaps back. The thing doesn't move after it collapses to the floor. Streaks of blood and brain matter have smeared the surface of the other apartment door. For a second you expect it to swing open, for your neighbor to appear and chastise you for the mess you have made. But it stays closed. Nobody home, it seems. None of the other doorways along the length of the hallway swing open either. Is the floor deserted? Are you the only one still here? Or are the others simply too frightened to show their faces? The question becomes meaningless as you feel your lunch churn in your stomach and then, without warning, it comes up and you find yourself bent over, retching. The sick feeling passes soon enough, though, and you realize that you have to get the hell out of here. Right now. Flee the city. Let the authorities get things under control. You can always come back later when things have returned to some semblance of normality.

You go back inside, grab your wallet and your keys from where you set them the night before on the coffee table before the couch, next to a pile of various magazines. Then you leave the apartment, close and lock the door behind you, try not to look at the dead thing lying near your feet. After taking a deep breath, you head toward the lobby at the end of the hallway where the elevators and the emergency staircase await.

If you decide to take the elevator, turn to page 14.

If you take the stairs instead, turn to page 18.

You think about opening the front door and taking the zombie down with a few well-placed shots of the handgun then decide you're not up to it. Not yet, at least. The idea of opening fire on a human being, or something that once *was* a human being, fills you with a deep sense of revulsion. You understand that at some point, if you plan on making it out of the city alive, you're probably going to have to overcome this squeamishness but figure you'll cross that bridge when you absolutely *have* to. Right now, you don't have to. There is more than one way out of this apartment, after all.

"I can't believe I'm doing this," you say as you head back out to the balcony, trying to ignore the sound of the zombie slapping at the door. You've got your car keys, which you grabbed from the coffee table in the living room, in your pocket along with some spare cash and your debit card. Tucked into the front of the jeans you are wearing, barrel pointed down, is the loaded handgun. In your front pocket is the box of spare cartridges. Around your waist you've loosely tied one of the sheets you've pulled off of your bed. In your hand you hold another one. The sheets are long enough to get you down two floors. In either of the apartments below you're going to have to gain entry, see if the main hallways along those floors are clear or not. Get more bed sheets if you have to. Not much of a plan, really, but better than going *mano a mano* with the zombie outside your door.

"I can't believe I'm doing this," you say again as you tie the sheet in your hands to the balcony railing. You test the knot once, twice, three times, assuring yourself that it's not going to give way at a crucial moment. And then, without thinking too much about it, you place both hands on the railing, carefully swing one leg over and then the other, grip the sheet as tightly as you can then carefully, oh, so carefully, start to lower yourself. At one point, your heart leaps into your throat as you're sure that the knot has slipped, as you await that feeling of freefall to the pavement far below. Maybe you'll get lucky and take a zombie out when you hit. But it's all in your head and the knot holds. Sweating and shaking, you eventually get your feet onto the railing of the balcony below yours. Moments later you've got solid concrete below your sneakered feet again.

"Damned lunatic," you mutter, trying to calm the rapid beating of your heart.

When you feel some semblance of calm returning, you turn and look through the sliding glass door of the person or *persons* residing one floor below you. You're hoping that whoever lives there has already vacated the place, decided to get out of Dodge long before you did. How much easier that would make things. You stand where you are for a good thirty seconds. It is darker inside the apartment than outside and the reflection of daylight off the glass makes it difficult to make out any details. At one point you think you detect movement then chalk it up to nerves and an imagination in overdrive. You should probably just go in, you tell yourself. Knock first, of course. Break the window if you have to. But what if there *is* someone in there? What if there's a zombie? Or more than one?

If you decide to descend one more floor, turn to page 16.

If you try to enter the apartment, turn to page 20.

As you reach for the handle of the front door, you cannot help but wonder if this is truly the wisest course of action. You're fairly confident, after all, that the undead creature standing outside the door is incapable of gaining entry into your apartment. You're rather amazed it ever made it up to your floor in the first place. Judging by what you've seen on the TV news reports, it would seem that the zombies are not the most intelligent creatures to ever walk the Earth. One might even classify them as brain dead. Mindless. Automatons. Wholly capable of zeroing in on potential prey, attacking and feeding upon that prey. But little else. It was also reported that individual zombies are not something that should generate any undue amount of fear. Only in packs are the creatures truly dangerous. One or two of them can be easily outrun. If you find yourself surrounded by a large group of them, however, you might find yourself in some serious trouble.

You are not in any immediate danger if you stay here. Once you set foot outside? Well, things are bound to get a whole lot more dangerous in a hurry, now aren't they? Hopefully the electricity will come back on at some point. And there is all that beer in the fridge. What can it hurt to stay one more night? Wake up early tomorrow, assess the situation. Undoubtedly, the authorities are doing what they can to bring the situation under control. Maybe by tomorrow...

So decided, you go into the kitchen, open the fridge, and pull out a beer. A little hair of the dog, that's what you need. No cheap stuff here either. No PBR or Busch or any of that nonsense. You like the good stuff. Imported wheat beer. A cold bottle of Franziskaner in hand, you open the freezer and pull out a frosted drinking glass. After pouring the beer and placing the bottle in the recycling bin, you circle the counter which separates the kitchen area from the living room and once again head out onto the balcony. Leaning on the railing, you take your time drinking your beer as you watch the spectacle unfolding below. People occasionally run by. Zombies shamble along. The smell of smoke reaches you, carried by on a light breeze. You cannot see a fire in either direction along the street where your apartment building is located. It has to be somewhere nearby, though. Another sign of the general decline of affairs in the city.

You finish the beer, go grab another, pass the time getting comfortably inebriated. At some point, you're not sure when, the zombie has stopped beating on the front door of your apartment. It seems that you've made the right decision after all. Stupid creature could never hope to get at you. Hell, a whole gang of them would probably be incapable of getting past that door. Looking down over the balcony's railing, you see a couple of zombies walking by in their slow, distinctive way. On an impulse, you grab one of the small potted plants you've been growing on a small metal shelf out on the balcony. Arm extended out over the railing, you take aim as best you can and let go of the potted plant. It falls the six stories and hits one of the zombies square on top of the head. You let out a whoop as the zombie collapses to the pavement. It does not get back up.

More drinking ensues. More dropping of plants. The morning has long since become the afternoon. Daylight fades slowly, imperceptibly towards night. The power does not come back on. The sounds of the nightmare that has overrun the city do not abate. Gunfire. Explosions. Screaming. Toward evening, you grab the flashlight you keep in one of the kitchen drawers then head toward the bedroom. There, you lie down, telling yourself that all will be better come morning. You fall asleep within minutes of lying down.

And awaken to the sound of some great beast roaring. There is a brief moment of utter terror and confusion. Are you actually awake? Is this some sort of nightmare brought on by the stress of the day? Then there is an explosion of light and heat. The walls of the room disappear. It seems as though your world has been consumed by a supernova. So much light. So much heat. There isn't even time to scream...

Wow. Apparently that whole zombie plague thing got a whole lot worse while you were sleeping. Became the sort of problem that someone with a lot of authority felt could only be solved with a really, really big bomb. You know, that's the problem with bombs like that. As long as they exist there's always someone just itching to set one of them off.

THE END

The floor's lobby is a small, square area with two sets of elevator doors before you and a gunmetal grey steel door to your right which leads to the emergency stairwell. Deciding to take the easy way, you press the down arrow button set into the wall between the two sets of elevator doors. It isn't long before the left hand set of doors slides open and you find yourself stepping into the empty elevator car beyond. Inside is a metal panel with two vertical rows of buttons numbered one through fifteen set into it. You reach out and press the button for the bottom floor and wait as the doors slide closed and the elevator car begins to descend. There is a digital readout above the doors which counts down the floors as you descend.

Five.

You still really can't believe any of this is happening. It's like a dream. A bad dream. The dead rising. All the terrible news footage. The walking dead man you had to shoot in the hallway.

Four.

Your stomach begins to churn once again as you recall, with far too much detail, the way the bullet had snapped the zombie's head back, the image of the insides of the zombie's head running down the apartment door.

Three.

You take in deep breaths, fighting the sick feeling threatening to steal over you again. It wouldn't do to go around throwing up all the time. You have to keep your wits about you. God only knows what other terrible things you may see and have to do next.

Two.

The sound of muffled screaming reaches your ears. It's an in-human sound. An animalistic sound. Not a sound of pain, no. Something else. Something more disturbing. It's the sound of mad-ness, complete and undiluted. A cold dread washes over you. With a trembling hand, you reach out and stab at the button marked with the number two, trying to stop the car's descent. It dawns on you that getting into this elevator may have been a very bad idea. You mentally will the car to stop, stabbing the second floor button repeatedly with your index finger. Shouldn't there be an emergency stop button? You're sure there is. In your panic, it takes you a few moments to notice the smaller metal panel next to the rows of buttons. There is a recessed latch on the panel which you pull at, opening it and revealing the button you are desperately searching for. But by then it is too late. The car is slowing, the number above the doors is reading:

One.

"No," you say, "oh, please no," as the doors start to open. There is that scream again. Much louder now, much closer and clearer. The doors open wider... wider... like a hungry mouth ready to feed. You back away as you see the crowd of shambling undead beyond and the one figure, in particular, at the front of the pack, standing there, looking into the elevator car with a look of such madness and twisted malevolence upon its broken facial features that you feel your bladder let go at the sight of it. And there is that scream again, emanating from the mouth of that hideous, ruined thing. A feeling of terror so pure it freezes the air in your lungs and takes hold as you silently cry out to whatever gods there may be to *please, oh, please, make the monster go away...* But it would seem that the gods aren't listening because the monster is rushing toward you, hands held out before it like claws. And the other zombies are closing in behind it. And soon the elevator car is crowded, far beyond its recommended capacity, and you start to scream yourself, a short lived sound as the undead do what they do and make a feast of the flesh of your body.

Obviously, this is not the way out of the city you were looking for.

THE END

Afraid that someone—or something—might be lurking within the fifth floor apartment, you decide to take your chances and descend another level. Acting quickly, you untie the second sheet from around your waist and repeat the same procedure you did outside your own apartment, securing the sheet as best you can to the balcony railing. You tug on it, assuring yourself once again that the knot will hold. And then it's over the railing, first one leg and then the other, but this time with a bit more haste. As soon as you commit your entire body weight to the bed sheet you are convinced once again that it is slipping. The only thing is, this time you're right. You are halfway down to the fourth floor balcony when the knot you've tied, the one you rushed, just a little, comes undone. With a shriek you fall, the bed sheet trailing upward behind you like a malfunctioning parachute. You roll over in midair and face the ground rushing up to meet you face first. And, guess what? You manage to land on one of the zombies, snapping its neck and driving it forcefully downward into the sidewalk. The undead creature breaks your fall, just a little. But not nearly enough to do you any good. At least your death wasn't a complete waste. There is, after all, now one less zombie to terrorize the city.

THE END

The idea of being trapped inside the elevator car does not appeal to you. Who knows what might be waiting on one of the lower floors, ready to enter that tiny room with you when the doors slide open? So you turn and head over to the grey metal door that leads into the emergency stairwell. It seems like the more sensible move as you can always backtrack if you run into a problem below.

The door closes behind you with a *clang* that echoes in the enclosed space more than you would like. You start downward, one cement stair at a time. At each floor there is a landing with mid-floor landings in between where the stairs reverse upon themselves. You set a brisk pace, not exactly running but not walking either. At each floor landing you stop and listen at the door that would lead out into the lobby area beyond. Then you open the door to see if there is any potential threat that you should be aware of. If a zombie could make it all the way up to the sixth floor then undoubtedly others could be on any of the floors below. At the third floor landing you stop again, hold the pistol out before you and pull the door open. What you see there causes your finger to tighten on the trigger.

"Whoa, whoa, whoa," says the man standing there, obviously quite alive, just beyond the open doorway. He is waving his hands in front of him in a warding gesture. You barely manage to keep from shooting the fellow as your heart races at this little surprise. Lowering the gun, you step backward into the stairwell, motioning for the man to follow.

When the door closes behind the man you offer an apology, tell him that you hadn't expected to see him there, that you're just a bit jumpy after... Well, after what you had to do outside the doorway of your apartment.

"It's all good," says the man with a hint of a southern, good ol' boy accent. He's a big guy dressed in jeans and a tucked-in tight black T-shirt. On his head is a well worn John Deere baseball cap. His hair is just long enough to pull back behind his ears. Around his waist is a black leather belt with a big shiny buckle. On his right hip you see a gun holster occupied by what looks like a much larger handgun than the one you have.

"Grant Tucker," he says, holding out his hand. You take it, offer a brief introduction of your own.

"Where you headed?" you ask after disengaging your hand from his.

"The hell outta here."

"Makes two of us," you tell him. "Probably should have gotten out sooner." You shrug. "Better late than never, huh?"

Grant laughs, claps you on the shoulder. "You got that right."

There comes the sound of a muffled scream from somewhere below, a piercing, inhuman bellow that conveys either an unthinkable level of agony or insanity. You and Grant exchange a look.

"What are you thinking?" you ask.

"I'm thinking that whatever made that sound, I don't want to encounter it. Might be one of those howlers they were talking about on the TV."

It could have been made by someone terribly injured, you argue. Someone in need of your aid.

The awful scream comes from below once again.

"Whatever's making that sound," says Grant with a shake of his head, "it ain't nothing we're gonna be able to help."

You're not so sure though. Even though it might be terribly risky to do so, a part of you thinks that you should go down and take a look. Quietly. Carefully. Grant says that the two of you should exit the stairwell at the second floor, break into an apartment and go out a window–the drop to the ground wouldn't be very far from there.

If you decide to go down and see what is happening in the lobby, turn to page 22.

If you agree with Grant and leave the stairwell at the second floor, turn to page 28.

You untie the second sheet wrapped around your midsection, let it fall to the balcony floor. Pulling the gun free from the front of your pants, you step forward, reach out and pull on the handle of the sliding glass door. To your surprise it slides open. You take a step into the apartment, stop and look around, wondering if you really had seen movement earlier. No one here now. Or if there is they may be waiting back where the bedroom and bathroom are located.

"Hello?" you call out, not wanting to startle anybody. When there is no reply you make your way through the living room over toward the front door. The place is laid out just like your place but is furnished quite differently. Abstract paintings adorn the walls as does a heavily loaded bookshelf. A stationary bike in the middle of the room is aimed in the direction of the TV. There is an exercise mat on the floor next to a collection of dumbbells. Whoever lives here obviously likes to keep in shape. You do too, to a certain extent, but you go to a local gym for your workouts. You call out again as you reach the front door. Still nothing. The gun is in your right hand, hanging at your side as you put your eye to the peephole and look out into the hallway beyond. No sign of any zombies out there. It seems that your little death-defying descent from the balcony was worth it. With a sigh of relief you pull away from the peephole and reach for the lock on the door.

"Who are you and what the hell are you doing in here?"

The voice comes from your right, in the direction of the short hallway that leads back to the bedroom end of the apartment. You turn to see a woman standing less than ten feet away dressed in nothing but a beige towel, long damp hair draping down over her bare shoulders. She appears to be in her mid-twenties, attractive, even with that look of seething anger on her face and the sawed off shotgun she is pointing at your mid-section. The arms that hold the shotgun are well muscled and you can see that the legs below where the towel ends are in good shape too. You freeze, try to look as non-threatening as possible, introduce yourself as the upstairs neighbor.

"Do me a favor and drop that gun in your hand."

You do as you're told.

"How did you get in here?"

You tell her. All of it. The zombie upstairs. The little trick with the bed sheet.

She barks a laugh. "Pretty extreme, let me tell you. And people say that *I'm* crazy."

"Crazy times," you say.

She laughs again, lowers the shotgun, just a little. "Well, how about us two lunatics make a run at getting out of this place together? I was about to give it a shot on my own. But, as they say, strength in numbers and all that."

You tell her that you think that sounds like a wonderful idea. You'd probably also agree that swimming in sewage sounds like a wonderful idea as long as that shotgun is pointed your way.

"I'm going to go and get dressed. It will only take me a couple of minutes. The name's Dora, by the way."

You tell her your name.

"All right. Be back in a few."

With that, she turns and heads back to the bedroom.

Turn to page 24.

At the second floor landing Grant grabs you by the arm, gives you a deadly serious look, and says, "Sorry, but this is as far as I go."

There is another horrible scream from below, a bit louder now, reverberating as it carries up the stairwell. You can't really blame Grant. The more you think about it, going down there isn't one of your brighter ideas. But the thought of leaving someone in that much pain... If you have to, you tell yourself, the least you can do is put the man out of his misery. Or maybe it's a woman, because, in all actuality, it's hard to tell.

"I'll just crack the door," you say. "Take a quick peek. If it looks too dangerous I'll turn around and get the hell out of there."

Grant pulls his big, shiny handgun out of its holster, says he'll go down one more landing. "You know, for some backup. But I'm not gonna to stick around long. Just lettin' you know that up front."

With that, you lead the way down the final flights of stairs, walking slowly and steadily, placing each foot on the next stair as softly and silently as possible. Again, that scream, all the louder now. It's enough to make you grit your teeth and cause your heart to pound more heavily in your chest. Grant stops at the final landing, gives you a nod of encouragement. You nod back then turn and make your way to the bottom of the stairs.

You place your ear to the door and hold your breath. Your mouth is dry as a summer drought. It feels as though your heart is on the verge of leaping out of your chest. At first there is nothing to hear. And then...

Moaning. Low and persistent. The same noise the dead thing outside of your door made. Then the scream comes again. The nearness of it makes you jump away from the door. A human being could not possibly make that sound. Not a living one. At least, you hope not. It was a mistake coming down here. Whatever it is that is making that awful sound beyond the door is something supremely dangerous. You can feel it in your bones. You start to turn away. It is the smart thing to do, after all. But what if you're wrong? What if someone in there really does need your help? Needs put out of his misery? As a child, you had entertained thoughts of becoming a doctor or maybe a veterinarian when you got older. You've always hated to see another living thing suffer. And whatever it is that is making that noise is undoubtedly suffering.

Seemingly of its own volition, your hand goes to the door handle. You turn it, slowly, slowly... Then you pull, ever so slightly, open it just enough, a fraction of an inch, place your eye to the crack in the door and try to see—

The door slams inward, hits you in the face, throws you backward, knocks you down into a sitting position. The impact dazes you. The gun in your hand slides across the cement floor. Then this... *thing* is on you. Pulling at you. Through your confusion you stare into its face with its broken features, its cooked nose and leering mouth, all wrapped in parchment white skin. And the eyes... In them you see the burning look of the damned... And a warped intelligence there. A barely functioning lunacy. The mouth opens and there is that scream. It pierces you, rattles around inside your skull. You try to push your inhuman assailant away, rather ineffectually, as the thing attacking you is possessed by some maniacal strength.

You hear a scream. A different scream. "NOOOO!!!" Then there is a terribly loud *booming* sound. Another. The thing on top of you cries out, stands up, starts to back away. You can hear Grant's voice shouting, "Get up, man. Jesus Christ, get up!!"

That's when the thing that attacked you charges past you and up the stairs. Grant fires his gun a couple more times. You start to get up but there are other hands grabbing at you now. The lobby is teeming with the undead. And now they have you. Looking around, you see your gun lying some five feet away over against the wall. Might as well be five miles away. You are pulled out of the stairwell and into the lobby. A single zombie you might be able to fight off. Maybe even two. But not this many. They surround you. Pull at you. Bite and bite again. Through your pain you wonder for a brief, flaring moment if Grant got away. Then there is nothing but agony, intense and overwhelming. Eventually, thankfully, there is nothing at all.

THE END

Dora reappears a few minutes later dressed in a tight black T-shirt, khaki shorts, a black belt, and a pair of light brown hiking boots. Her well-muscled arms and legs are displayed to full effect. She drops a large black duffel bag at her feet then ties her hair back in a ponytail.

"Ready to do this?" she asks, taking the duffel bag in her hands again.

"Yeah. Sure thing," you tell her.

She smiles. "Let's go then."

Out in the hallway she sets off at a brisk pace toward the small lobby at the end of the hall. You follow. Without hesitation, she walks past the elevator doors and heads toward the emergency stairwell. Then she surprises you by heading *up* the stairs instead of down.

"Where are we going?" you ask.

"To the roof."

"And why are we going to the roof?"

"You'll see. We'll be there shortly."

You don't doubt it, with the pace she's setting. In practically no time at all, the two of you reach the top of the stairwell. You're breathing a bit heavily after the nine story ascent. If you live through all of this, you tell yourself, you're going to have to start hitting the gym more often than you have been in recent weeks. Dora isn't winded at all. She may have just gotten up off the couch from all the fatigue—or lack thereof—she's showing.

She reaches out, tries the handle of the door that you assume leads out onto the roof. It refuses to turn. This actually relieves you a bit as you're not at all certain you want to find out what she has planned for the two of you if and when you get past that door. Seemingly unperturbed by this minor setback, she reaches into a front pocket of her shorts with her free hand and pulls out a ring of keys. Selecting one from the dozen or so on the ring, she uses it to unlock the door and pushes it open before returning the ring to her pocket.

"Why do you have a key to the roof?" you ask, genuinely curious.

She laughs. "Terrence, the old superintendent, he had a bit of a thing for me. We used to come up her on occasion and... well... smoke a little weed, maybe drink a couple of beers. I talked him into letting me have a duplicate of the key so I could come here if he wasn't around. He ended up getting fired about a year back. Not sure where he ended up. Nice enough guy..."

She walks out onto the roof which is covered in a fine sort of gravel which makes a crunching sound beneath your feet as you walk. A low wall, only a couple of feet high, runs around the perimeter of the roof. Dora leads you over toward the south side of the building, the side you cannot see from your balcony. As you approach the edge, a group of pigeons takes flight from where they were perching on top of the wall. About five feet from the wall, Dora stops and sets the duffel bag at her feet, crouches down and unzips the bag. Reaching in, she pulls out a pair of handguns, sets them next to the bag. Your knowledge of firearms is fairly limited but you think you can recognize a couple of Glocks when you see them. The fact that Dora owns something like that does not come as much of a surprise to you. In the brief time that you've known her, you've gotten the impression that she would be prepared for just about any situation that comes her way. And you've seen and read the reports that explain how every year more and more of your fellow citizens seems to be arming themselves. With all the bad news coming from the media these days, who can blame them? And there's always the fact that you never can tell when you might wake up one day and find yourself in the midst of a full-blown zombie apocalypse.

Next, Dora pulls out a clear plastic Ziploc bag filled with a number of protein and energy bars. Then comes the canteen which she clips to her belt. And finally, she removes two red, rectangular packs with a series of straps attached to them. The sight of them gives you a sinking feeling.

"Are those..."

"Yeah, they sure are," she says as she stands up and hands you one of the packs. "Parachutes."

"You can't be serious."

"Oh, I can be," she says with a smile that contradicts what she tells you. "And I am. Base jumping is serious business. Do something wrong and you can get yourself killed in a hurry."

"I can't..." you start to say. She gives you a look. "What I mean is, I've never done anything like this before. Base jumping. Parachuting. Hell, I've never even bungee jumped. I'm not really much of a risk taker."

"What about that little balcony trick?"

Yeah, there is that. More the exception than the rule, though.

"Look," she says as she uses the straps to attach the parachute to her back. "There's nothing to it. Do exactly as I tell you, and you're gonna be fine. Now turn around and I'll help you put it on."

If you chicken out and head back into the building, turn to page 30.

If you decide to follow Dora's lead, turn to page 36.

Along the second floor hallway you and Grant start checking doors. You knock on the one you approach. Grant doesn't bother. You can hear him rattling doorknobs as he tries to gain entrance to the even numbered apartments while you work the odds. You are at the third door, apartment 205, when you feel the doorknob turn in your hand. You knock again, a bit more loudly this time, just to make sure no one's home before you push the door open.

"I got one," you call out to Grant who's almost reached the end of the hallway by now.

"Ha!" he cries out, followed by: "Got one here too."

It seems that there is no shortage of people who've forgotten to secure their homes in their haste to flee the city. The door that Grant has opened leads into an apartment on the same side of the building as the place where you live. You recall the view from your balcony. No shortage of zombies wandering around on the street out there. The apartment that you have gained entrance to will have a window leading out to the parking lot behind the building. Maybe the scene isn't quite as chaotic out there. Maybe. Hopefully. Plus, your car is out there. It might be better to try and leave town behind the wheel of your sporty little Nissan two door than on foot. Before you can say any of these things, Grant calls out, "Let's check this one out!" and disappears through the unlocked door he has discovered.

"Oh, wonderful," you mutter, not at all happy with your newfound friend's rash behavior, wondering if you might be better off attempting an escape on your own.

If you tell yourself the two of you should stick together, turn to page 32.

If you decide to ditch Grant, turn to page 40.

You look out toward the city, see the tops of some of the smaller buildings nearby, think about just how far of a fall it is to the ground those fifteen stories below. You feel the breath catch in your throat and all of your muscles tense up at the very idea of it. The image of the chute not opening runs through your mind... the sheer, screaming terror as you plummet to the ground... the sickening, crushing, deadly impact at the end of the fall...

You back away from Dora. Obviously, she's crazy. Anyone who would contemplate such a maneuver *has* to be crazy, doesn't she?

"I can't do it," you tell her. "Sorry."

You turn and hurry back toward the doorway that will take you into the stairwell and down from the roof. Just being up here is causing a mild sense of vertigo to fill your head.

"Suit yourself," you hear Dora say.

Inside the stairwell, you stop and lean with your back against the wall, taking in deep breaths, willing the dizziness that so suddenly came on to dissipate. And, eventually, it does after a few minutes of being back inside. The thought of falling is a bit of a phobia with you. Standing on the balcony of your apartment, you're fine. The railing is there, after all. Something protecting you from the drop beyond the balcony's edge. The thought of falling never really enters your mind there. But out there on the roof... With all that openness around you... The idea of leaping out into that openness... It was all just a bit overwhelming. You're a little embarrassed at your cowardice but at least you are alive to feel that way, you tell yourself. You hope everything works out for Dora. She seems like a nice enough person. But in the end, you're all about looking out for number one. And your idea of looking out does not involve leaping off the roofs of very tall buildings.

Feeling like you've got your bearings again, you start making your way back down the stairwell. The thought of running into any of the undead sometime along your descent frightens you almost as much as what Dora would have had you do. But you've got your gun. And you know that you'll use it if you have to. And at some point, you figure, it's more than likely that you'll have to.

The weight of the .38 feels good in your hand, sturdy and reassuring. Zombies can be shot. They can be killed, once and for all.

Guns do little good against headlong falls from the roofs of apartment buildings.

So telling yourself, you reach the stairwell's eleventh story landing–

The door there bursts inward and a man dressed like an accountant–white button up shirt and a pair of navy blue dress pants–appears in front of you, gun in hand. You have a moment to think, *Jeez, I guess everyone in this town really* is *armed.* And then the guy pulls the trigger. The shot punches you in the chest, right through the heart. A good shot. A killing shot. As far as actual living human beings are concerned. A shot like that, though, probably would have done very little to stop a zombie.

The .38 drops from your hand and you fall headlong onto the landing. The guy who shot you stands there saying, "Oh, my God. Oh, my God. You're one of them, right? You have to be one of them..."

Then he is kneeling next to you, reaching out and touching you, saying, "Nononononono..." And you can't help but think that the guy must be some sort of idiot, because if you were "one of them" you'd be able to reach out, as close as he is, pull him down and have yourself some dinner. Or lunch, considering the time of day. But the thought is fleeting because there is so much pain. And shock. And so much blood pouring out of the hole in your chest. It spreads quickly beneath you, a pool of it that soon covers half the landing.

"I'm sorry," the man is saying. "Without my glasses... I thought you were a zombie... coming at me..."

Oh, for want of a pair of glasses...

That one last, absurd, fleeting thought.

Then the world goes black. The pain goes away. And...

Nothingness.

THE END

"Grant, wait up!" you say and head down to the apartment into which the guy had entered. Number 212. The door is hanging open and Grant is there in the living room.

"Now this is what I'm talking about!" he says.

You wonder what has him so exited. And then you see. On the same wall where you have the TV in your apartment so does the resident here. But next to it, instead of an area of empty space, is a small bar. Grant is already circling around it, getting a closer look at the myriad of bottles on the shelves there.

"Hey, hold on a minute," you say.

He turns and gives you a smile. "What's up?"

"Are you even sure there's no one here?"

"I called out. Got no answer."

"That doesn't mean we can just help ourselves to whatever's in the place. Maybe whoever lives here is on their way back."

"I'm thinkin' probably not. Way I see it, they got excited by something goin' on outside, went out for a closer look. And, *bam!* Zombie food. Or maybe they got turned into one of the disgusting buggers."

"But you don't know that. You just can't start taking–"

"It's just a drink. That's all. Don't tell me you can't use one."

Now that he mentions it... You're still feeling the after effects from the night before. A little bit, at least. You've never been prone to hangovers, as long as you get enough sleep. And you definitely got enough sleep last night. But still, a little hair of the dog might do you good. And besides, what's really the harm? The damn city is being overrun by the undead. You don't think anyone's going to get too worked up about a couple of guys helping themselves to a little booze. The thought of all those zombies wandering around out there... how much they'd love to get a taste of your warm, living flesh... the things you may have to do to make your way out of this hellish city...

You sigh. "Make it a double."

"Oh, now we're talking."

It isn't long before Grant and you are clinking a couple of glasses filled with top shelf bourbon together. "To the two baddest zombie killers this town's ever seen," he says and downs his drink.

You're not so sure about all that. The memory of the way you reacted after shooting the zombie outside your apartment is still much too fresh in your mind. And you have no idea if Grant's even killed a single zombie as of yet. But it hardly seems the time or place to express your doubts.

"I'll drink to that."

And you do.

Afterward, you slam the glass down on top of the bar and shiver noticeably. The stuff went down like some sort of concentrated diesel fuel.

"Now that hit the spot," says Grant and, much to your incredulity, he pours you each another shot.

"I don't know," you say. It comes out in a sort of wheeze.

"Come on. The last one, I promise. It's not gonna kill you."

Another *clink* and another upending of the whiskey glass. This one doesn't go down any easier. As you stand there, one hand on the bar for support, taking in deep breaths, Grant swings out from behind the bar and disappears down the apartment's hallway in the direction of the bedrooms. You know it's useless to argue with him so you let him go. Instead, you make your way out onto the balcony and survey the scene outside.

Not much has changed since you took in the view from four stories above. There's still a lot of the shambling dead out there. As you watch, a guy on a bicycle rides by on the sidewalk across the street, one hand gripping the handlebars, the other firing a pistol indiscriminately at any nearby zombie. His aim is not very good as none of the zombies go down. The man seems to be enjoying himself well enough, though; you can hear his high-pitched laughter from where you're standing. It seems that the whole damned world has gone insane. Or, at least, the whole damned city.

A few minutes go by and then Grant is behind you saying, "Take a look at this."

In his hands are a couple of weapons you've only seen in the movies.

"Are those..."

"That's right. Uzis. Whoever lives here's got himself a whole damned arsenal back in the bedroom. Probably one of them gang banger types. Or a survivalist."

"In an apartment building? In the middle of downtown?"

He shrugs. "It takes all types, don't you know?"

"I suppose."

He hands you one of the Uzis. "Box of clips back there too. Let's pocket a few and do this thing."

The booze and the feel of this new weapon in your hand is doing some interesting things to your attitude concerning the whole situation in which you've found yourself. Maybe you and Grant *are* the baddest couple of zombie killers this town has ever seen. Really only one way to find out, right?

By the time you're ready to leave, you have a pistol in your belt, an Uzi in your hand, a box of cartridges for the pistol in your front left pocket, and a replacement clip for the Uzi in each of your back pockets.

"Ready to rock'n'roll?" asks Grant. He's got a grin on his face that lets you know how *he* feels. Unbelievably, you find yourself grinning in return.

"Ready as I'll ever be."

Turn to page 62.

You don't like this. Not one bit. The fear of falling... It's a big one for you. As a child you were forced onto one of those "Tower of Terror" rides, the kind that lifts you straight up into the air to a great height and then drops you... And just like that, the damage was done. You were crying when you got off the thing. And you never rode it again. Never got on a rollercoaster either. That falling sensation... It makes you break out in a mild sweat just thinking about it.

Dora can see you hesitating. Maybe she can see the fear there too.

"I promise, I won't let anything happen to you," she tells you. "As far as the jump goes, I mean." She smiles. "After that... Well, we *are* in a city overrun by zombies."

You take a deep breath. Another. *You can do this*, you tell yourself. You think about this falling phobia. A childhood fear. But you're not a child anymore. Are you? No. You've outgrown many childish things. Other childhood fears. Why not this too? Yeah, why not? And there's really only one way to overcome a phobia, or so you've heard. You have to face it. Meet it head on. Defeat it. And never look back.

You give Dora a determine nod. "Let's do it."

She reaches over and pats you on the shoulder. "Now that's what I like to hear."

She helps you into the harnesses that attach the chute to your body. And then she's pulling a leather belt out of the duffel bag, tightening it around her waist above the other belt she wears. There is a holster on each side of this second belt. Into each of these she deposits one of the Glocks.

She goes over the proper way to deploy the pilot chute and then the chute itself, how to control the direction of your fall once the chute has opened. She tells you a second time, has you repeat it back to her.

"Piece of cake, huh?" she asks.

Your throat is dry but you manage to say, "Yeah, piece of cake."

"Now I'm going to go first. I'll be aiming for the strip of grass at the far side of the parking lot. After I go, you count to five Mississippi and follow. Got it?"

"Got it."

And then she's leading you over to the building's edge, stepping up onto the flat surface on top of the low wall there. "Tell me again. Tell me what you're going to do once you leave the roof."

You tell her. It all seems simple enough. As long as you don't panic you should be able to pull this off. And you are not going to panic. No more childish fears... At least that's what you keep telling yourself.

She turns her head and looks back at where you are standing only a few feet behind her, gives you a wink. "Piece of cake," she says again. "See you on the ground."

With that, she leaps off the roof in a graceful swan dive. Your heart is beating heavily in your chest, threatens to burst free as you watch her take that jump. Your bladder feels tight and suddenly you can't breathe. You haven't been counting. How many seconds have passed. Two? *Three Mississippi*, you tell yourself.

Fighting the panic that now threatens to grip you, you place one foot on top of the wall.

Four Mississippi.

You try to breathe.

No more fear.

No more fear!

No more fear!!

The city stretches away before you. And there is Dora, chute open, drifting out and over the parking lot below. She makes it look so easy. So graceful. Maybe it really *is* a piece of cake.

A brief moment of calm settles over you, like the eye in the hurricane of worry and panic and doubt swirling around you. A brief moment where you can breathe again. The sky above you is so clear and bright. You smile. Crouch down. And leap outward with everything you've got.

And then you are falling... falling... Time becomes simultaneously compressed and extended. A second goes whipping by, seems to stretch on and on forever... Another second...

You release the pilot chute, just like Dora told you to. Then the main chute deploys with a violent flapping sound. And just like that, your plunge toward the Earth is abated, converted into a more leisurely and manageable glide. You grab the handles that dangle just above your head–again, just as Dora instructed–and attempt to steer yourself in the direction that Dora went before you. You can feel the fear, the old childhood phobia, fighting to take control of your mind again. But it has weakened. The worst is over. You remembered to deploy the chute. You did not panic and plummet to your death. This part of the ride is actually quite enjoyable. You look down and see the parked cars, the few that are left, that were not taken by those who have already tried to flee the city, passing by beneath you–there's your sporty little two door right there! A small number of the undead meander between the parked cars. They look like robots that have malfunctioned, wandering about aimlessly, with no purpose at all. You're sure that they'd remember their purpose, however, if you happened to drop down next to one.

You raise your eyes and lock in on the patch of grassy ground where Dora is landing right at this very moment. If you were to continue on your present course, you'd overshoot the designated landing area, drift out into the street beyond. You're too high, too far to the left. The panic threatens to return.

Relax. Breathe in... and out... Remember what Dora told you.

Using the handles, you turn yourself a little to the right. A little more. Then you slow your forward momentum.

And here it comes, the patch of grass that separates the parking area from the street beyond. It's maybe a dozen feet across. A small target for an inexperienced jumper like yourself. But you've made it this far... Might as well take it all the way.

You turn a little more to the right. Then you are slowing... slowing... Bending your legs and...

There's the landing! Not all that pretty, no. You pitch forward and end up sprawled on the grass, facedown. The parachute comes down and trails out behind you like some sort of monstrous, deflated egg sack. Then there are hands on you, strong, firm hands that help you to your feet, brush at the grass sticking to your shirt.

"That was great!" Dora says and she hugs you. You have to agree with her. That *was* pretty great. You can't believe you actually pulled it off. Dora releases her hold on you, goes to work repacking the chutes as you stand guard, your pistol drawn. Let the zombies come. They can't hurt you. Right now, you feel as though nothing can.

Dora is quite adept at what she is doing and has the chutes re-packed in only a few minutes. No zombies come to harass you while she works, disappointing you, just a little.

When she is done she lifts the packs and leads you over to a car that is parked nearby in the lot. A black, BMW convertible. She extracts her key ring, disarms the car alarm with a beeping sound, pops the trunk and tosses the chutes inside. Then she pushes the trunk closed, turns to you and says, "So what do you think? Shall we make our escape on foot? Or by car?"

If you think it is a better idea to set off on foot, turn to page 42.

If you'd like to get out of town in that sleek BMW convertible, turn to page 50.

Forget that guy, you tell yourself. You're better off on your own anyway. If he changes his mind and wants to follow, that's fine. No *way* you're going out the front of the building where you know the zombies have gathered *en masse*. You step through the doorway and into apartment 205. The place has been almost entirely cleared out. A couple of padded metal chairs, the kind you might find around someone's poker table, have been left in the middle of the living room area. Also, a painting of a wilting flower has been left hanging on a wall, slightly askew. It looks so lonely there. Dispirited. Abandoned.

You head across the room toward the sliding glass doors. The blinds have been pulled shut and so you take a moment to open them. You pop the lock on the door then push it open. Then you are out on the balcony, surveying the scene before you.

You breathe a sigh of relief at the lack of activity out here. You can see a few figures meandering about between a couple rows of parked cars. But nothing like the zombie mayhem you previously witnessed taking place on the building's other side. You lean out over the balcony's edge and look down. The drop to the stretch of grass below is very doable. Within moments you are climbing over the railing, crouching down and finding a grip on the edge of the balcony's cement platform, lowering your legs and then just letting go. Stumbling a bit as you hit the ground, you drop to a knee before popping back up and pulling free the handgun tucked into the front of your jeans. You take a minute to replace the replace the bullets you fired earlier with fresh ones from the box of cartridges in your pocket. Then you head off in the direction where you parked your car. It's a short jog and luckily no zombies have to be confronted along the way. As you get into the vehicle, you set the gun onto the passenger seat before putting the key in the ignition. Backing out of the parking spot, you tune the radio to a local talk station.

"—advising residents who have not yet left the city to stay put," says the voice emanating from the car's speakers. "Authorities are doing everything within their power to bring the situation under control. It is much more dangerous to be out of doors under present circumstances. Keep your doors locked and the radio on for more information. If you find that you must venture out into the

streets, stay away from any slow moving packs of people. Also, be sure to avoid those who seem to take little notice of any life threatening injuries they may have sustained, or are wandering about while screaming incoherently. These are symptoms consistent with those in the early stages of the infection. These howlers, *as they are being called, will try to spread the virus by first physically attacking a healthy individual then exhaling a dark breath filled with contagion into the face of that individual, according to eyewitnesses. To repeat, government officials are advising—"*

"Yeah, screw that," you mutter and head toward the parking lot's rear exit. It is soon apparent that you have made the right choice as the street before you, which runs north and south, parallel to the one you gazed down upon from your balcony, appears to be relatively free of undead activity. The building where you live is near the heart of the city and so hanging a left (northbound) or a right (southbound) will lead you on a journey of approximately the same distance to the city's perimeter.

If you decide to go north, turn to page 46.

If you hang a right instead, turn to page 54.

"Streets could be crowded or possibly blocked," you say. "I think we should take our chances on foot."

From the look on Dora's face you think she's about to argue, but then she just shakes her head and says, "Sounds like a plan. Let's head out."

The two of you walk away from the parking lot. The road which the lot exits onto is Elm which runs in a north-south direction. Dora seems to think that the city's border is a bit closer to the south so that's the direction you go. As you approach the first intersection at 4th St. N., the rumbling sound of an explosion from somewhere else in the city reaches you. A sense of unease starts to mingle with the feeling of euphoria you've been experiencing since the jump off the apartment building. Dora's silence isn't helping. Her head keeps darting back and forth, scanning the faces of buildings lining the road, apparently searching for any signs of danger. She has a Glock in one hand, the muscles of that arm tensed as if ready to aim and fire at the first provocation. So far, there are no signs of the undead which is good, isn't it? For some reason, however, the lack of a zombie presence only feeds the anxiety taking root within you.

"So what's your story, Dora?" you ask in a rough voice barely more than a whisper. You have to do something to help take your mind off the feeling of dread threatening to settle over you. A little conversation might do the trick.

But Dora's answers are short and forced. Her dad had been in the military. Did some work in Hollywood as a stuntman for a while. Taught her some of the stuff he learned along the way. She got into martial arts before her teens. Met a guy who was into base jumping some years back. Fell in love with him. Traveled around the world doing all manner of jumps with the guy. Until his chute didn't open one day. She decided to get her nursing degree. Ended up here, working at the local hospital. And that was that...

More silence. At least, between the two of you. But from other parts of the city, near and far: Screams. Awful howling sounds. Gunfire. An alarm beeping away. More explosions.

At Elm and Central, the two of you finally run into the trouble Dora has obviously been expecting. From the west, a great, moaning pack of zombies. Like a tide rolling in, they crowd the street a block away, stumbling and shambling inexorably toward you. The smell hits you even now, a vanguard announcing the undead presence, just in case it somehow escaped the attention of your eyes. It is a thick and heavy odor, the sickly sweet scent of rot, carried on an easterly breeze to where you and Dora have stopped momentarily to watch. And then, from the south, comes a pained screaming sound. More zombies there, walking into the next intersection from the west, two figures leading the pack with a strange agility and a quickness unmatched by the zombies behind them.

"Howlers," you say remembering the TV report you were watching a short while ago.

"This way," says Dora with a light tug on your arm. And she sets off in a jog to the east.

Oak St. is at the next intersection over. You see a car enter the crossroads there from the north, hear the squealing of breaks as it comes to a sudden and skidding halt. There is a crunching sound as a large chunk of rock slams into the car's windshield. And then two more of those faster moving, howling creatures approach the car from the south. The driver, in a panic, puts the car in reverse and squeals the tires in an attempted getaway. But he veers too sharply to the right, smashing into a parked car at the corner of the intersection. The howling figures waste no time in rushing the vehicle. One of them is holding something in its hand–it looks like a golf club from this distance–and takes a swing at the driver's side window. As you watch this scene unfold, a loose group of zombies enters the intersection and approaches the car currently under attack.

You and Dora come to a stop halfway along the roadway between Elm, behind you, and Oak, before you. Looking back over your shoulder, you can see the mass of zombies there coming closer. And the two howlers there... They come around the corner and start to head along Central directly toward you. One of them screams and they break into a near sprint. Looking back toward the wrecked car, you see more zombies entering the area but the crowd there is not as thick as the one behind you. And they seem fairly preoccupied with finding a way into the car.

"Any ideas?" you ask as your heart beats heavily in your chest and your mouth goes dry with fear.

Dora looks behind her, then toward Oak, then behind her again. You can see the indecision there. But no real fear. This is one tough lady you've teamed up with. For that, at least, you can be grateful.

"The way forward is our best bet," she says. "Not as many of the awful things in that direction. But I think we're going to have to–"

She is cut short by a wholly unexpected sound, a metallic, scraping sound coming from nearby. No more than ten feet away, as a matter of fact. You look down and see a manhole cover which has been lifted and is being pushed aside by somebody underneath. When the heavy lid is completely clear of the opening, a man's head pops up and out of the hole in the ground, swivels one way and then the other. "Ah, shit," you can plainly hear the man say. Then he is reaching for the cover, starting to pull it back into place as he lowers himself back into the hole.

"Hey, wait, you son of a bitch!" shouts Dora and she rushes the opening.

You follow her across the short distance, come up behind her as she stops and aims her Glock down into the hole, at the face of the man peering up from the dark opening into the light above. "We're coming with you!" says Dora, the tone of her voice and the gun in her hand making it clear that this is a statement not open for argument.

"Fine, fine," says the man and he disappears down into the darkness of the hole. "But you better be quick. Damn howlers'll be on you in no time. And make sure you cover the hole after you're in."

Dora turns and looks at you, motions with the gun. "Go on, get in there."

Then she walks back toward the approaching mass of zombies.

"What are you–"

"Giving us a little time," she says. "Now go!"

The two howlers are close, not even ten yards away, and coming fast. The one on the left, a woman, is covered in blood. The one on the right is a teenage boy who appears to have been scalped Old West style. Dora walks toward them with a confident stride, raises her arm and starts to fire. Not waiting to be told again, you lower yourself into the hole. It is basically a cement tube with metal rungs set into it, each of them a foot and a half apart, forming a ladder. There is a dank, musty odor coming up from some undetermined distance below. You hear a few more bursts of gunfire from the street above and then look up to see Dora peering down at you. You're maybe ten feet down when she puts her booted feet on the metal rungs and follows you down. She takes the time to pull the metal cover into place, grunting a bit at the effort involved. Then the cover settles snugly into position like a lid on a pot, plunging your surroundings into total darkness.

Turn to page 58.

You hang a left, head northbound, and give the little sports car some gas. The street that runs along the front of your building is Magnolia. This is Elm. All the north-south roads in this part of town are named after trees, which are, quite noticeably, in relatively short supply around here. The east-west streets are numbered, counting up from central a few blocks south of where you live. You approach the intersection at Fifth, see that the light is blinking yellow. It seems that the electricity is out here too. Good thing nightfall is still a ways off. The place is going to be awfully dark when that happens. The thought of being out here among all the zombies with such limited visibility... You feel a chill work its way down your back.

Reaching over, you turn off the radio, cutting short the repeated warning urging people to stay indoors. You think about putting on some music but decide against it. Best to have as few distractions as possible. You're surprised and a bit relieved to discover that the streets here are relatively zombie free. A couple of figures can be seen near the sides of the road and over on the sidewalks, but so far you haven't had to swerve to avoid running over one of the walking dead. Keeping the car's speed at a steady thirty miles per hour, you approach the intersection at Sixth and Elm. And that's when you run into your first bit of trouble. A school bus is on its side just beyond the crossroads, completely blocking any further northbound progress. Without wasting too much time thinking about it, you put on your blinker–some habits never die, it seems–and turn right. Then it's over to Oak St. and another blinking traffic light. There you turn left and give the car some gas.

Just then, a man seemingly appears from out of nowhere, directly in front of you, waving his hands in an effort to get you to stop. It's not the gesture that makes you stop the car but the fact that if you don't turn immediately you're going to run this idiot over. So you turn, right into a car parked on the side of the road in front of a bakery. The impact is violent enough to inflate the airbag and shake you up just a bit. Steam rises from beneath the hood. Not a good sign. Looks like the car isn't going to be drivable after this. especially with the airbag deployed.

"Sonofabitch," you mutter.

There is a knocking at the driver side window. Turning your head, you see the guy you almost ran down standing there, leaning over so he can look in at you. The window is up so you reach over and press the button on the door that lowers it.

"Wow, I'm really sorry about that," he says. Up close, you can see how young he is. Early twenties at most. Dressed in shorts and a T-shirt. Backwards baseball cap on his head. "Are you all right?"

You tell him, "Yeah, I think so. And what the hell did you think you were doing jumping out in front of the car like that?"

He offers a sheepish grin. "Couldn't think of how else to get you to stop. Just looking for a ride out of this godforsaken place."

It's then that you realize the seatbelt doesn't want to unbuckle. "I'm stuck," you say, pulling at the unyielding restraint.

"Oh. Damn. That's not good." The kid's grin falters. "You got a knife or... I don't know... something to cut yourself out of there with?"

You start to tell him that, no you don't have a knife or anything else that might get the job done. But the kid interrupts you with an, "Oh, Jesus," before turning and running away.

"Hey!" you shout. "What the hell?"

You don't want to think about what scared the guy off like that. But how can you not think about it? And it doesn't take a genius to figure out what it probably was.

Feeling the first sharp edges of panic setting in, you pull harder and harder against the safety harness, try to duck down and maneuver your head underneath it. But the combination of the belt and the airbag are doing a rather commendable job of trapping you where you sit. It isn't long before the first sounds of moaning reach you through the open window. That's when the fear really takes hold. After closing the window, you look over to where you had set the handgun on the passenger seat. It's not there. Of course, the sudden stopping of the car resulted in the gun being thrown onto the passenger side floor, well out of your reach. Unless you can get free of the safety harness, that is.

You punch at the airbag, curse and pull at the seatbelt with everything you've got. It's becoming more and more obvious that you're not going anywhere unless you find something with which to cut yourself free.

Once again, you hear the sound of knocking at your window. A duller sound than before. That's because it's a zombie knocking this time and it's using an open hand instead of a fist. The lone zombie is joined by another and then several more. It isn't long before the entire car is surrounded. They beat at the windows, the roof and the hood of the car repeatedly, the sound morphing into a ceaseless pounding like that of a hailstorm assaulting the vehicle. In your fear you tell yourself that they haven't the strength to break the windows nor the intelligence to use some sort of tool—say, a tire iron or a baseball bat—to gain entrance. But then there is the sound of the passenger side window imploding. You look and—*Oh, come on, you've* got *to be kidding!*—see a guy with a hole in his face where his nose used to be, dressed in a jersey with some local softball team's logo printed across the front of it. And, guess what? He's got a bat. And, apparently, he knows quite well how to use it. Some habits die hard indeed.

After that, it all happens pretty fast. The door is opened and one of the zombies climbs into the car. You punch at the undead creature a couple of times but then it just leans in and bites a nice big chunk out of your biceps muscles. You've known pain before but never anything like this. Following dead softball guy's lead, another zombie finds something that it uses to cave in the driver's side window. And then the feast is on in earnest. Yeah, it all happens pretty fast. But not fast enough. No, not by a long shot. Certain things, like being eaten to death, they just seem to go on and on forever.

THE END

"I'd really rather not try to get out of the city on foot," you say. Dora nods her head in agreement, as if certain this would be your answer. "But, from what I saw on the news, a lot of the roads are blocked. Driving could prove equally as difficult."

"But a bit safer, wouldn't you say?"

"So it would seem."

"And, not to toot my own horn, but I've done a bit of professional driving in my day."

"Why doesn't that surprise me?"

She laughs. "Get in. I'm feeling an urge to get out of this place as quickly as possible."

Moments later, you're belted into the passenger seat of Dora's BMW. The engine starts with a healthy purr. She backs the car out of the space, weaves around an approaching zombie, heads for the lot's exit.

The street before you heads north and south. Without asking, she turns to the right, heads southbound toward the river a few miles off. It's a natural barrier, doesn't have the heavy military presence that the eastern perimeter has where checkpoints have been set up at every road leaving out of town. It doesn't need it. That is, if the news reports are correct.

"Most of the evacuees will be headed east, I'm sure. They'll flock toward the presence of authority. Shouldn't run into as much traffic this way. I think there'll be less zombies, too. Less people to feed upon."

It's a grisly thought but you can't argue with the logic.

And it seems that her reasoning is correct. You pass only a few other vehicles as the Beamer zips along the mostly deserted streets. Dora easily avoids any of the walking dead who shamble out into the road in front of the vehicle. She handles the car like a real pro, all right. You can't help but wonder where she learned all these unique skills.

"From my father," she tells you after you pose the question. "He did some time in the military. Saw action in Vietnam. When he got back he went west. California. Hollywood, to be exact. Found work as a stuntman on some low budget films. Turned it into a fairly lucrative career. He married an actress from a B movie shoot he was working. Knocked her up. Was hoping to have a boy. Straight up told me that. Said that he loved me anyway and was still intent on making me as tough an SOB. as he could manage. I spent a lot of time on set with him. Started taking martial arts when I still wore my hair in pigtails. Took stunt driving courses when I was old enough to get my license. Then I met a guy who swept me off my feet. He was totally nuts. Loved to base jump. Freakin' *loved* it. We went all over the world. Jumped off anything we could climb up onto. Got arrested a couple of times. One time, his chute didn't open..."

She is quiet for a minute. The car hums along. You don't know what to say.

"I took it hard. My dad, he told me to head back out to L.A. He'd get me a job. So I went there. Two days later he's diagnosed with cancer. It killed him in less than a year. And after that... I just lost the heart for stunt work. It was my dad's thing, you know. That was seven years ago. My mom remarried last year. I bounced around from job to job, all of it pretty boring stuff. Went to school and got my nursing degree. Was offered a job at one of the local hospitals here a little more than six months ago. And, well... That's about that."

The car approaches an intersection showing a red light. Dora slows, comes to a stop. It seems that the electricity is working here. Must be on a different grid from the one that feeds your apartment building.

"So what's your story?" she asks.

Ahead and to your right, on the southwest corner of the intersection, sits a church. It's made of red brick with a wide wooden door and a white steeple. A white cross adorns the wall above the doorway. *No shortage of churches in this town*, you tell yourself.

Just as you start to answer Dora's question and share a little of your own background with her, the door to the church flies open and a woman comes running out and down the short flight of wide, stone stairs that leads to the sidewalk at the edge of the road. The woman starts waving her hands frantically in the direction of Dora's BMW. You can see that she is shouting something but you cannot hear what it is from inside the airtight confines of the vehicle.

The light turns green and Dora zips through the intersection, pulls over near the corner and the frantic woman.

"What are you doing?" you ask, not sure if stopping and helping the woman is actually the wisest course of action. You'd really like to get out of town as quickly as possible.

"This will only take a sec," she says. "Can't leave behind a woman in distress."

Who knew your newfound friend had such a big heart?

She opens the door and exits the vehicle. Sighing, you do the same.

Dora approaches the woman with her hands out in a calming posture. "It's all right. It's all right," she says. "Just tell me what's going on."

"My father. The pastor," says the woman, her eyes filling with tears. "He's inside. I think it may be a heart attack. We were preparing to leave and he collapsed. I don't know what to do."

"I know CPR," says Dora, laying a reassuring hand on the woman's shoulder. "And I've had some first aid training. Lead the way."

The woman turns and hurries back into the church. Dora follows. After a moment's hesitation, you follow the two women inside.

The interior of the building is dimly lit. After the brightness of the afternoon outside, it takes your eyes a few moments to adjust to the gloom. In that time you hear the heavy front door swing shut behind you. Turning to see who closed the door, you realize that the woman and her father are far from the only ones here. No, there are a good dozen people standing to either side of the door through which you have just entered. More than a few of them are armed. And about half of those weapons are pointed right at you, the other half at Dora who's standing only a few feet away.

"Great," you mutter, not all that surprised by events taking a sudden and profound turn for the worst.

The room you are in is about thirty feet wide by fifteen deep. You're in the building's narthex. A couple of empty coat racks stand near the walls. A flight of stairs leads upward to a second floor, and a smaller doorway directly opposite the main entranceway leads into the sanctuary beyond. You look toward this second doorway, see the woman who lured you into this place standing there.

"What's this all about?' asks Dora. You can hear the anger in her voice.

Just then the interior doorway swings open and a tall, elderly man dressed in the robes of a priest steps into the room.

"I see you have found our... guests of honor... for tonight's ceremony," he says.

"Yes, father," says the woman now standing next to him, the one you came to help.

"Very good." The old man's voice is raspy with age. "As I have told you, my children, the Lord works in mysterious ways. But he always does find a way." He smiles. "After you have searched them, bring them inside." With that he turns and heads back into the church. A few armed men approach.

"Hands up," one of them says. You comply. A few moments later, Dora does too. You are frisked quickly and efficiently. The .38 is confiscated. So are Dora's weapons.

"Please, come inside," says the pastor's daughter and she heads off in the same direction as her father. Having little choice in the matter, you and Dora follow. The others fall in line behind you.

Turn to page 66.

You turn right, heading south. Reaching over, you turn on the radio, flip through some stations along the AM band, hoping to hear anything interesting. A few of them repeat similar warnings: If you are still in the city then it is best to stay indoors. Remain calm. Officials are doing everything they can to bring the situation under control. Do not venture outside unless it is absolutely necessary.

Besides trying to get the hell out of town, you have to wonder what event would arise to make it "absolutely necessary" to head outside while the undead are overrunning the city. You can only think of a few. If your house is on fire, you suppose. Or the zombies have entered your home. Or if you've run out of beer. No one could hope to ride out a zombie apocalypse without any beer...

The traffic in this direction is relatively light. In fact, it's practically nonexistent. It seems that coming this way was a good idea. Most of the people, you assume, are heading east toward the greatest concentration of military personnel. Which means most of the zombies would be headed that way too, undoubtedly, in pursuit of the fleeing humans. Zombies have gotta eat, after all.

The first intersection you approach has a flashing yellow light. You do the proper thing and slow, proceed with caution. Two intersections later and the lights seem to be working. From a distance you can see that it is green; as you get closer it changes to red. Apparently the electrical grid is still functioning here. The realization gives you hope. Ahead, you see three people emerge from a townhouse set into a row of similar structures on the right. The last person out turns and fires a handgun back in the direction of the door from which he—at least you think it's a "he" from here—has just emerged. Moments later you understand why as a pair of slower moving figures exit the building. The man with the gun fires again and the first of the slower figures—it seems rather apparent that the two newcomers are of the undead variety—collapses to the ground. The man fires again and the second zombie staggers but does not go down. One of the two people who emerged from the townhouse with the gun toting man comes up behind him, reaches out and pulls on his shoulder. The gesture is obvious: time to go. You don't wait to see the outcome of the little drama playing out before you. Instead, you look to your left, see no approaching traffic, and hang a right. At the next light you hang a left, not wanting to venture any further in the direction of the spreading gas cloud that triggered this whole mess in the first place. A block ahead and the buildings on both sides of the road are on fire. The true extent of the situation in which the city finds itself is demonstrated in the lack of fire trucks or any other type of emergency vehicle at the scene. No doubt, the vast majority of emergency workers have already fled the city, been infected or killed, or are busy with more pressing situations elsewhere. The destruction of a city block by fire seems to take a back seat to other affairs when the streets are overrun by the walking dead.

You drive ahead at a steady but cautious pace. The air is thick with smoke and although you can still see well enough to drive, your vision is limited enough that you don't want to take a chance driving at excessive speeds. No sense in doing anything stupid at this point of the game. Just keep moving forward and heading south. It shouldn't take you too long to reach the river at the city's border there. Get over one of those bridges and the worst is behind you. That is, if the news reports are to be believed. You flip through a couple AM stations hoping to hear some updated information. But there is a lot of interference here. Would the smoke be causing that? Or is it just one of those areas where the radio signals have a hard time of it? You've encountered such areas before. Hopefully things will clear up as you near the river.

As you reach the end of the block you hear a great roaring sound and, startled, you look into the rearview mirror just in time to see one of the buildings behind you—all five stories of it—collapse and crumble outward into the street. You try not to think about what might have happened if you'd come this way only a few seconds later. *Just keep moving*, you tell yourself. Pondering what might have been does you no good at all.

At the next intersection the lights are all blinking yellow. A van sits waiting to your right, aimed in an eastbound direction. You wave the vehicle through as it clearly has the right of way. It doesn't move. Perturbed, you give the horn a gentle beep, motion again for the van to move along. And still it just sits there.

"Fine," you mutter. And proceed out into the intersection. That's when the van decides to go. Whoever is driving the other vehicle punches the gas, causing the tires to squeal as the van—a plain white thing that looks to carry about twice the mass of your own vehicle—leaps forward and slams into the passenger side door of your car. The impact causes your shoulder and the side of your head to slam up against the window to your left, momentarily dazing you. As your car comes to a rest you try to gather your wits and make some sense of what just happened. Then, to add to your confusion, there comes a banging upon the window beside you. Looking out, you see a man standing there, dressed in a long-sleeved black shirt with the sleeves rolled up to the elbows, a dark blue knit cap on top of his head and a doctor's mask obscuring the lower half of his face. Oh, yeah, and he is also pointing a rather large looking black pistol at you through the window.

"Open the door!" he shouts, motioning toward the door handle with the gun he is holding. "Now."

As you don't seem to have a whole lot of choice in the matter, you comply.

"Now get out. Take a couple steps to your left... That's it. Hands out in front of you where I can see them."

The way he talks makes you think he has issued similar orders before, like he is a police officer. But then there's the doctor's mask. Although he could have gotten that anywhere, couldn't he? And the things he's telling you—could have picked them up from any number of police dramas or movies he may have seen.

"You got any weapons?"

The world seems to be straightening out once again. The side of your head hurts though and it feels like there might be some blood trickling down past your ear. You think about lying to the masked man but there is something in his eyes, the way they seem to dart back and forth a little, a wild, nervous energy that makes you think otherwise. No telling how he might react if he discovers the untruth.

"Yeah. Tucked down the front of my pants."

He steps forward and in a quick motion lifts your shirt, grabs the butt of the .38 and pulls it free. "Any more ammo?" Within moments he has the boxes of cartridges too. "Good, very good." He pops open the cylinder of the .38, closes it again. Then he tosses his own gun backward over his shoulder.

"Hate to do it to you," he says then offers a shrug. "But desperate times and all that."

He swings the barrel of the gun to your left and fires. Aims to the right and fires again. As the sound of the weapon's retort echoes away down the streets in either direction, you can hear the unmistakable hissing sound of air escaping the tires of your car.

"Good luck to you then," says the man. And with that he backs away, keeping the barrel of your .38 aimed at your midsection, circles around the car and out of sight behind you. The van, which had been left idling during the entire ordeal, accelerates in reverse after you hear the sound of one of its doors swinging open and then closed. And just like that the masked man drives away. Leaving you unarmed and on foot in the south side of a city which has become a feeding ground for the walking dead.

This is a section of town you're not all that familiar with but you're pretty sure that the river runs only a half dozen or so blocks south of where you're standing. The air surrounding you is thick with the smell of smoke. Bringing your hand up to the side of your head, you touch the matted hair there and look at your fingers, the tips of which are red with blood. The wound doesn't seem to be all that serious, though, probably only a minor cut. You know from past experience that head wounds tend to bleed more than similar afflictions to other areas of the body. Nonetheless, it's something you should probably have looked at as soon as possible as you may need a couple of stitches. Cursing the masked man and wishing some terrible fate to befall him, you start walking in the direction you were driving, ready to run as fast as your legs—still a bit wobbly—can carry you at the first sign of trouble.

Turn to page 74.

So now you're in the sewers. Go figure.

The journey down was longer than expected. Must have been a couple dozen rungs on that damn ladder, each of them slippery with condensation. You almost lost your grip once or twice, made the trip down to the bottom a lot faster. But you're here now. The guy who opened the manhole cover is standing a short distance away. He's got a flashlight. It's on with the beam aimed down toward the ground. Dora drops the few feet from the ladder's bottom rung, lands on the ground next to you. She turns and now both of you are staring toward the guy with the light. He's staring back at you, not saying a word, as if deciding what it is he should do with you. Hard to make out his features in the weird lighting but from what you can see—and what you saw up on the street for that brief moment—he seems to be a fairly young person, not yet middle aged. Scruffy, dark hair protruding from beneath the kind of wide brimmed hat you might see on a guy who makes his living deep sea fishing. His white T-shirt is stained to the point of not being very white anymore. Baggy black pants tucked into a pair of rubber boots and a backpack, complete his ensemble. With a shake of his head he turns and heads off down the damp corridor in which you now find yourself. "Come on then," he calls back over his shoulder.

You and Dora exchange a look in the rapidly failing light. She shrugs and heads off after the man. Seeing as how you don't seem to have much of a choice in the matter, you do the same.

We're heading south, you tell yourself, trying to keep track of the direction you're walking. *Toward the river.* Unsurprisingly, it stinks down here. It is an arched, brick corridor through which you walk, maybe seven feet high. Water drips from the cracks in between the bricks and runs down the walls in rivulets, giving the passageway a glistening, sweaty appearance. You can hear rushing water from beyond the wall to your right. In sections, the ground is covered in a couple inches of stagnant water and your shoes are quickly soaked through. The tunnel branches. Branches again. And again. You get the impression that the passageway through which you are walking is curved in places. It isn't long before you lose all sense of direction.

"Where are we going?"

It's Dora who asks the question, the first thing that's been said since the three of you set off on this little journey.

"Home," says the guy without looking back, his voice echoing along the corridor.

"Home?" you wonder aloud.

"Not far now," comes the response.

More silence. More branching of the corridors. A further loss of direction.

At one point, you cross a narrow metal bridge with a rusted railing to either side. About ten feet below rushes a murky river. The stench is something not to be believed. You find yourself gasping, trying to clear your lungs as you enter another arched corridor and leave the sound of rushing water behind.

"Almost there," says the man.

The corridor opens onto a wide, square room about fifty feet to a side. The ceiling disappears into the gloom above. The floor here is constructed of metal grates. The sound of gurgling liquid comes up from below. Archways are set into each of the rooms four walls, a rusted plate over each marking them 1, 2, 3, and 4. You have just entered the room from the archway marked number three.

Good thing it wasn't number two, you tell yourself, trying to find comfort in some sophomoric humor.

In the center of the room is a great machine, twenty feet tall if it's an inch, all bulbous metal sections and long metal tubes disappearing down through the grates in the floor. The machine emits a steady mechanical hum.

In three places around the machine are metal barrels with fires burning in them. There are at least a dozen people gathered here, some of them standing together in groups, others drinking or eating by themselves out of brown lunch bags. The clothes they all wear are stained and ratty looking. No one looks like they've had a bath in a long time

As your guide approaches a group of these people, one of them calls out, "Hey, Art, were you able to get any smokes?"

Art shakes his head, says, "Nope. Dead bastards were everywhere. Got us some newcomers, though."

Nobody says anything, just stares in your direction.

"Good to meet you too," says Dora.

"This is where you live?" you ask, shocked in spite of yourself. Sure, you've seen TV shows about this kind of thing, but to see it firsthand, in person...

Art turns and looks at you. "Here and other places beneath the city."

"My god..."

"It's not so bad," he says with a grin. "Especially in the winter. Freeze your ass off topside."

"Damn, I sure could use a smoke," says the person who previously addressed Art.

"I'll try again in a little while," says Art. "Just a matter of going up at the right place."

Dora approaches Art, says, "Any chance you can lead us toward the river. We're trying to get out of the city. I've got money."

Art's eyes light up. "Sure. I can take you straight *into* the damned river if you want."

This gets a laugh from those standing nearby.

And then there comes another sound. Distant. Barely audible. The echo of an echo. Emanating from the tunnel that brought you here.

Howling.

Dora raises a hand. "Shhh." Silence falls, except for the whirring of the machine. And that other sound, not so distant now, the howling.

"We've got company," she says.

And then, more howling, much louder, much *closer*, from the number one tunnel.

"Oh, no," says Art.

A couple of shambling figures suddenly burst out of the darkness of the number one tunnel.

"Time to go," says Dora.

The number two and number four tunnels seem to be your safest options.

Dora says, "This way," and heads toward the number two tunnel.

You've got a strange feeling, though. Number four is the way to go. Call it survival instinct. Sixth sense. Whatever. Something is telling you to head that way. The way to safety.

If you tell Dora that you think she should follow you, turn to page 96.

If you shake off the feeling and follow Dora toward the number two exit, turn to page 170.

The two of you clamber over the railing, lower yourselves down, stand on top of the other railing which encloses the first floor patio of the apartment below, then jump down to the ground near the sidewalk that runs alongside Magnolia Ave. And just like that, you're in the heart of it.

The place is practically crawling with the undead. It has always been one of the busier sections of roadway in this part of the city and the onset of armageddon has done little to change that. Zombies limp about in groups or alone. Across the street someone runs by screaming. As soon as you and Grant hit the ground you attract the attention of a good dozen or so nearby zombies. They turn toward you and start to come your way.

"Let's do this!" Grant shouts as he raises the Uzi in his hand, steps toward a nearby pack of the walking dead, and squeezes off a short burst of annihilation. The spray of bullets catches a trio of zombies square in the face. Chunks of skull and hair and barely functioning brain matter rip free of their heads. They go down. Grant is laughing, high-pitched and hysterical. You figure it's time to join in the fun and so you mimic Grant and squeeze off a spray of projectiles toward a couple of zombies before you. The gun doesn't kick like you expect it to but the combined energy of so many escaping rounds forces your aim to ride up. Several bullets fly across the street and smack into the wall of the building there, shattering one of the windows. But the two zombies are down and you find that you're laughing too. Grant is firing again, telling you to only squeeze off short bursts.

"Damn guns eats bullets," he is shouting. "Don't wanna waste 'em."

The carnage that ensues is impressive, to say the least. In less than a minute the two of you have cut a clearing that encompasses about half the block you're on. Bodies lie everywhere. There are a couple dozen, at least. You're down to the last cartridge for the Uzi. After that it will be back to the handgun.

"Ok, let's move," says Grant. And he heads off to the right. Northbound. As you pass by the entrance to your apartment building and the lobby beyond, you see that the glass doors have been shattered. The lobby is filled with the undead. They must have recently found some food in there, you surmise. Some unlucky, living SOB's must have gotten trapped. The promise of fresh meat would have proven an irresistible lure. This is pure speculation, you know, in no small amount fueled by the alcohol coursing through your bloodstream. But the theory feels right. And until you're presented with a better one, it's the one you're going with. Grant is a few steps ahead of you, moving at a brisk jog. You're just past the entranceway when you hear a scream emerge from inside the lobby that makes you quicken your step. Grant, though, has stopped, is turning back to see what's going on.

"What the hell was that?"

You come up beside him and turn to stare at the shattered doorway. Moments later, you see just what, exactly, the hell that was.

It's no ordinary zombie that emerges from the entranceway, that much you can tell immediately. There is something different in the way it carries itself. Something in the way it looks at the two of you. A noticeable agility in the way it walks, not the slow shambling of the others. Like it's not really dead at all. There is a cold, calculating look in the stare it levels at you. A burning madness there. That looks causes the breath to stick in your lungs for a moment. Your mouth goes dry with fear.

"A goddamned howler," says Grant from where he stands beside you, a faint quiver noticeable in that watered down southern drawl. "Has to be. I had the radio on. They were talkin' about 'em."

"There was some mention on TV about them too. Supposed to be extremely dangerous."

"Well, so am I," says Grant, his Uzi held out before him but not firing. Not yet.

The thing is about twenty feet away. It takes a few more steps toward you then stops. Zombies limp out of the doorway behind it. There is that scream again, issuing from the mouth of the insane thing standing before you. So much pain in that scream. Like some proud creature now badly broken and left to die. And not just physically broken.

"It's aware of what's happening to it," you tell him, not sure how you know this but certain you are right. Something in those eyes... "It can *feel* it. Somewhere, deep down inside, it knows what it's turning into. And its mind has snapped at the realization."

"Yeah, I guess it would," Grant says after a moment.

There is another scream. The thing opens its crooked mouth—jaw obviously broken on one side—farther than a normal human jaw should ever open and lets loose that terrible sound again. It doesn't move, allows the others to approach it from behind, to begin to encircle it.

Now Grant says, "I guess we should be the ones to put it out of its misery, huh?"

"Yeah, I guess we could do that."

You raise your arm, point the Uzi at the crowd gathering before you.

And that's when the howler moves, backward, into the surrounding mob, just as Grant and you burn through the remainder of your rounds and lay the crowd of undead low. In the aftermath of this slaughter, you see that the insane thing is not among the now unmoving dead. It must have slipped back into the lobby of the apartment building during the mayhem.

"Damn, that thing was quick," you say. "And definitely intelligent."

You toss the now useless Uzi to the ground, pull the handgun from your belt. Grant produces a pistol of his own.

"Let's get the hell outta here," he says. "Stick around much longer and we're sure to end up as zombie food."

The two of you keep heading in the direction you were previously traveling, northbound. It isn't long before you jog up to an intersection with a blinking traffic light. This is the intersection of Magnolia Avenue and Fifth Street North.

"So which way then?" asks Grant, rather surprisingly as he has, so far, taken the lead on this little expedition. Nice of him to let you make the decision here, although you have no better idea than he does of the direction you should go.

If you decide to turn right and head east on 5th St N., turn to page 70.

If you turn left and head west on 5th St N., turn to page 76.

If you continue north along Magnolia Ave., turn to page 122.

You and Dora follow the pastor's daughter down a wide aisle between two deep rows of pews. The air carries hints of some mellow perfume, incense possibly, a touch of vanilla in its scent. The ceiling arches high overhead, disappears into the gloom there. The place is so serene, so quiet. The cough of one of your captors reverberates throughout the place. Looking left and right, you picture the pews filled with parishioners, heads bowed, offering up their thanks and platitudes to the Good Lord Who Art in Heaven, amen. If only they knew that the man leading them in their prayers, that the daughter of that very man, were both capable of holding those who sought to offer them aid against their will. What would they think then? Would they still follow the man in prayer?

The aisle ends before a wide set of stairs that leads up to a stage about four or five feet above where the worshippers sit. There is a pulpit there with a microphone attached to it. Behind the pulpit is a tub where baptisms are undoubtedly performed on a weekly basis. Before the wall above and behind the tub is a giant statue of Christ the Savior on the cross. To either side of this representation of terrible cruelty and suffering are tall, rectangular, stained glass windows through which a red and yellow and green tinted light streams into the place, currently the cavernous room's only source of illumination. The atmospheric lighting casts the suffering Christ in an eerie glow. He wears nothing but a tattered loincloth. The hollows of his ribs and abdomen, the tightly stretched muscles of his arms and legs stand out in all of their painstakingly crafted detail. The wound in his side is a gaping thing, terrible to behold. Beneath the weeping wounds caused by the crown of thorns upon his head, his eyes are only partly opened. The agony portrayed there is a nearly palpable thing. Those eyes, they seem to bore into you, to accuse you. Overcome with a mild sense of superstitious dread, you look away.

You and Dora are brought before the pulpit where you are ordered to stop. Your captors fan out behind and around you. The old pastor ascends the short flight of stairs, circles around and stands behind the pulpit, looks down upon the two of you with the wide and glaring eyes of a vengeful messiah. Or a crazed zealot.

"Do you know why you are here?" the old man asks of you. The mic and the church's PA system are not turned on but the pastor's voice reaches you easily, casts echoes throughout the sprawling, silent room.

"Because you forced us to come here?" says Dora, a mocking tone of defiance quite evident in her voice.

"Yes, there is that," says the pastor and he chuckles. "But more, so much more."

Dora sighs. "There always is."

"Silence," says the pastor's daughter from where she stands on the stairs, to the right and slightly below her father. "You will only respond to a direct question from the Redeemer."

"Redeemer?" asks Dora. "From what does he offer redemption?" She laughs. Guns click all around the two of you.

"I said silence!" shouts the pastor's daughter. *Silence, silence, silence...* echoes the last word.

You nudge Dora with your elbow. She gives you a look, turns her attention back to the preacher. Fortunately, she says nothing further.

"You were brought here," says the pastor, as if the recent interruption never occurred, "to save the city from its current peril. For a time, at least. For a time."

You're not at all sure that you like what you're hearing. Not that you figured you would, after being held at gunpoint the way you have been.

"The Lord, he speaks to me, you see. Very directly. Very succinctly. He has spoken to me since a very early age. Since I was a child. He told me he had a plan. For me. For the world. He recently told me what that plan was." He pauses, takes in a long, dramatic breath. "As of this day, the first part of that plan has been set in motion. The end times... They are upon us. This is only the beginning. A sign. A warning. Soon, many will perish. Many more than have fallen on this day. So many more. Only the devout, the chosen, will survive. Those willing to do what must be done to help usher in a new age for mankind. To create a Heaven down here on Earth. To create a world finally worthy of the presence of its creator."

"Amen," a number of people say from the crowd surrounding you.

"Right here, within the walls of this church, we will show the Great and Mighty Lord Above that *we* are the devout, that *we* are, in fact, the chosen. That we are willing to do what must be done to usher in that new age. But first, before the Creator can be welcomed among us, the Earth must be cleansed of its countless sins. The time is upon us. The first sign of the apocalypse has been revealed. The dead have risen. They walk among us. And they must be laid low... Last night, in a vision, the Lord showed me exactly how this must be done..."

The old priest pauses in his ranting to stare first at you then at Dora before continuing: "Now do you know why you are here?"

"Ummm," says Dora, clearly exaggerating her befuddlement. "Not really. But seeing as how you guys are the *chosen ones* and all, and given that all these guns are pointed at us, I'm assuming it's not something either of us are going to enjoy a whole lot."

You do have to admire her devil may care attitude.

"To *enjoy...*" says the pastor, drawing the last word out. "You see, that's part of the problem. Too many people simply *enjoying* themselves these days. In ways they should never enjoy themselves. The drugs. The violence. The unbridled carnality of it all. It's an affront to all that is holy. It's an affront to God himself."

"He told you this?" Dora interrupts. Someone jams the butt of a rifle into her back. With a grunt she stumbles forward, drops to a knee.

"Yes, he told me this!" The pastor raises his voice. "And more. So much more. He told me that the dead will rise. On this very day. That it was a sign. The first sign. And that a sacrifice would have to be made. A pair of sacrifices. And that the lambs would be led right to our door."

"I knew I wasn't going to like this," Dora manages to say.

"No! Don't!" says the pastor, presumably to whoever was about to deliver Dora another blow. "Like it or not," he continues, "it is the Lord's will. And His will shall be done. Take them away."

Dora is pulled to her feet and the two of you are led past the first row of pews, around the stage to a simple wooden door set into the wall there. Someone turns on a flashlight and you are guided through the door, down a dark, windowless hallway with a number of other doors set into either side. Halfway down the hall you are told to enter a small, bare room with white walls and a tiny, frosted window maybe a foot across, set high into its back wall through which flows a dull stream of light. Then the door is closed behind you and audibly locked from the other side.

"Well, this is a fine mess we've gotten ourselves into," says Dora with a noticeable strain in her voice.

"Yeah, as if dealing with that whole zombie apocalypse thing wasn't enough."

You watch as she paces around the enclosed area for a bit. Back and forth, back and forth, like a caged animal, muttering under her breath all the while.

"So what are we going to do?" you ask, hoping she may have some sort of plan forming within her mind.

Dora stops pacing and looks at you. "What *can* we do?" she asks, obviously struggling to control her anger. "Bust out of here? Kick down the door? Try and take them by surprise?" She laughs. There is no humor in the sound. "Either that or wait until they come for us, see what it is they have in mind." She starts pacing again.

Neither idea sounds like a very good one.

If you say, "To hell with it, let's bust out of this place," then turn to page 82.

If you keep quiet and wait things out, turn to page 142.

You decide to head east toward the heaviest military presence. If things are going to be under control anywhere then you figure that's the most likely area. Apparently roadblocks have been set up along every roadway leading out of the city in that direction. A major undertaking if ever there was one. Not that you blame the Powers That Be. Obviously, what's happening here within the city cannot be allowed to spread beyond its borders.

Rows of townhouses line the street here to either side. You pass a man and a woman loading the back of an SUV with a couple of suitcases. Further along, you watch as a man buckles a young girl into the passenger seat of a pickup truck. Then he starts up the vehicle and races back in the direction from which you've just approached.

"Even a truck's not gonna to do him much good in this mess," says Grant from where he walks beside you. "He won't get far."

The idea of trying to get out of town on foot is obviously a good one. Sure, a vehicle offers some protection against the undead monsters wandering the streets. But, like Grant said, there are just too many obstacles in the way. Too many closed roads. You'd end up driving around in circles or backtracking more than actually getting anywhere.

The intersection you approach is an exception to the rule, however. It is relatively clear of traffic. Two cop cars sit at the corners, red and blue lights flashing on their roofs. A pair of police officers stand in the middle of the intersection directing traffic. They wear helmets, goggles, body armor over their uniforms. Not that the gear is actually going to do them much good in the face of a zombie horde. As far as you know, the zombies don't use guns and, therefore, aren't going to be taking any shots at the officers. But, hey, protocol is protocol, you assume. And whatever makes them feel safer...

"Good day, officer," shouts Grant as the two of you cross the street just to the right of the intersection after checking to make sure the way is clear of cars, or anything else that might cause you harm. From here you can see that the cops have pistols in their hands, much as you and Grant do. But they also have rifles strapped across their backs. They don't say anything in reply. Just give you a look and a nod, then go back to... Well, as there is no traffic here at the moment, whatever it is they are doing.

"Couple of Nervous Nellies," says Grant with a grin.

And who can blame them? you wonder.

"Pretty damn brave, if you ask me," you counter. "Just the two of them, out here, all alone, doing their jobs."

"Ha!" Grant's not buying it. "They're just followin' orders. Probably weren't given a choice. Maybe they got bribed with some serious hazard pay."

Whatever. All you know is that you wouldn't want to have to do their job.

You're thirty yards or so past the intersection when you hear one of the officers say, "Aw, shit. We got company."

Looking back, you see a pair of zombies wander over toward the officers in their slow, hindered way. The cops raise their guns and fire one after the next: *pop-pop!* The shots are true and the zombies collapse to the pavement.

"Nice shootin'," says Grant.

"Yeah, looks like they've had some practice."

You approach the next intersection, this one clogged with stalled and abandoned cars. At the corner is a convenience store, its front doors hanging wide open. If you had to guess, you'd say some looting had taken place there.

"Damn, I could use a smoke," says Grant. "Quit a year ago, but let me tell you, the urge is back on me somethin' fierce."

With that he heads over toward the convenience store.

"Hey! Where are you going?"

"Relax," says Grant with a wave of the hand. "Just seein' if anyone left any cigarettes behind. Be back in a jiffy."

He disappears through the open front door of the store.

You wait out on the sidewalk, cursing the man's impulsive behavior. One of his stunts is going to get the both of you killed at some point, you're pretty certain of that. And just as you tell yourself to not overreact—

"Oh, no," you hear Grant say from inside the store. "Oh, Jesus!"

Now *that* doesn't sound good.

If you run into the convenience store to see what's going on, turn to page 88.

If you decide to stay right where you are, turn to page 104.

As you walk the scent of smoke starts to fade. The second intersection you come to has working lights. A stream of cars flows through in an easterly direction. You have to wait for the light to change, and hope all the while that people are still in the right frame of mind to obey the rules of the road before you can cross. Along the next section of road, fronted only by buildings on the right hand side—mostly various stores and shops—you encounter the occasional wandering zombie. As you pass each one of the creatures you can hear them moan as they turn in your direction, reaching out toward you. Giving them a wide berth, you find yourself in no immediate danger. Along the left side of the street here is a tall, black fence made of iron posts topped with spikes. Near the middle of the fence is an even taller, arching gateway. A driveway leads in beyond the gate toward a sprawling, red brick manor. One would have to assume that whoever it is that resides there would feel quite safe during the present troubles. No doubt, a fence like that would prove more than adequate to keep the zombies away. Even the more agile, howling creatures loose in the city.

At the next street corner you see a rather unexpected and disturbing sight. A young child, hardly more than an infant, comes stumbling into view wearing nothing more than a pair of dirty underwear. Its skin is filthy and bruised and appears to be marred by several open cuts. In its tiny hands it holds the severed foot of a much larger person. The appendage ends in a ragged stump, just above the ankle. The child is chewing on the heel of the foot, completely oblivious to your presence. You stop and stare as the zombie child wanders by a mere dozen or so feet in front of you. Shuddering, you continue on your way once the little monster passes.

A couple more blocks and you're convinced you can smell the river. It's a subtle but rather pleasant odor, much preferable to the heavy smell of burning buildings you've left behind. The undead are a thicker presence here but their numbers are still not enough to alarm you. They wander about individually, aimlessly, like lost pets having no idea which way will take them home. You do have one brief scare as a pack of five zombies comes out of an alleyway just as you walk by, reaching out and turning in your direction, their voices rising in a shared moan, a seeming request for you to please stop, don't run away, allow us to feast on the warm, living flesh covering your bones.

You run away.

And finally, eventually, you are there. The road you've been following joins another street running in a north-westerly direction, parallel to the river beyond. At the side of the road is a cement walkway and a black metal railing that separates pedestrians from the thirty feet or so of the grass decline that runs down to the edge of the river. At the railing, you look out across the expanse of flowing water before you. There are houses built along the bank on the other side. But they seem so far away. You're a pretty good swimmer but wading out into that dark current holds little appeal for you. There have been a few recent storms and there's no telling just how strong the current might be. Plus, you have to wonder if the dark waters are much of a deterrent as far as the undead are concerned. Sure, it would be extremely difficult for them to reach the far bank given their rather limited motor skills. But surely some of them would be stupid enough to enter the river anyway. Might there be some of them out there, floundering about within the dark waters, awaiting a chance encounter with someone swimming by above them, at which point in time they could just reach up and pull the unfortunate swimmer down into a watery grave? The very idea causes your heart to beat a bit more heavily in your chest. You decide to head off in search of another, safer way to cross the river before you.

If you turn left and head in a southeasterly direction, turn to page 86.

If you turn right and head in a northwesterly direction, turn to page 100.

"This way," you tell your companion, and head west. You don't get three steps before you feel a hand on your arm and Grant is turning you to face him.

"Whoa, there. Now wait a minute."

"What's the problem?" you ask and shake his arm free, a bit more roughly than you intended.

"I'm not so sure that this is a good idea."

"That what isn't a good idea?"

"Goin' this way. You know. Toward the source. Toward the lab where all this shit started."

"Well, I wasn't planning on heading all the way over to where all the trouble began. Just figured that if we head that way..." You jerk your thumb back toward the east. "Then we're bound to run into some heavy traffic at some point. Because that's the direction everyone else is going to head, away from the source of all the trouble, over toward the bulk of the military presence."

"I guess you've got something there."

"I'm thinkin' we head this way a couple'a blocks then swing north and make a break for the river there. If things start to look bad, we can always turn around and head back the other way."

Sure, there is some added risk to the plan, moving toward the heart of the disaster, but the logic of what you've just laid out seems pretty sound, even when spoken aloud. Although, it is completely possible, you realize, that the couple shots of whiskey inside of you may be hampering your judgment ever so slightly. Any bit of self doubt, however, is crushed by the slap on the shoulder Grant gives you and the big grin spreading across his face.

"All right, let's do it then," he says.

And with that, the two of you head west.

You stay on the sidewalk, close to the fronts of the office buildings that line the street there. And, for a while, your plan seems to be working out quite admirably. Most of the traffic, vehicular and pedestrian, is moving in the direction opposite that in which the two of you are moving. Staying close to the wall keeps you out of the way of those walking toward you. Cars beep at one another, urging each other through intersections where the lights are not working and there is no one to direct traffic. A police car sits at one of the crossroads you pass through, lights spinning on the roof. The two officers inside the car, however, seem to be in no hurry to come out and try to maintain some sense of order. Not that you can really blame them. The air is thick with fear and tension as cars cut in front of one another, their drivers making every attempt to get out of town as quickly as possible. Pedestrians keep their gazes straight ahead and their mouths closed, ignoring any strangers they pass, which include you and Grant. Your new friend seems to find some humor in this for he laughs and calls out to a couple of women walking by: "A beautiful afternoon for a stroll, isn't it ladies?" They say nothing, seem to wrap their arms more tightly around the few possessions they carry, lower their eyes and quicken their steps.

"*Now* the urgency sets in on them," says Grant shaking his head in bewilderment. "Should have left town hours ago, if they were smart."

"Can't say we're any smarter than they are," you say, feeling some small urge to defend the frightened people scurrying by.

Grant laughs. "But at least we're havin' some fun with it."

You don't have a response to that. By now you're really starting to wonder just how mentally sound your travelling companion may be. And what of your own psychological state? After all, you're the one leading him deeper into the nightmare that has overrun the city.

Only a couple more blocks, you tell yourself. *Then we'll head north. Should be smooth sailing from there.*

On one of the corners at the next intersection, a man stands next to a shopping cart, holding something up in the air. "Gas masks!" you hear him shouting as you get nearer. "Get your gas masks! Only fifty dollars a piece!"

"Fifty dollars?" says Grant with a note of incredulity in his voice. "Quite a deal. Must have found 'em stolen somewhere. Probably not a lot of buyers, I figure. Pretty obvious that not many people are heading in the direction where they're gonna need 'em."

As you come up near the guy, you can see that the shopping cart next to him is filled with the black masks with their long snouts and clear plastic eyes. He's a tall, young fellow with a long goatee and a head full of black hair pulled back in a thick ponytail.

"Gas masks! Only fifty bucks. Best deal in town!

You figure you'll just keep on walking past the guy but Grant stops before him and, wondering what he might be up to, you stop and turn to watch the proceedings.

"How about a little two-for-one special?" asks Grant, reaching into his pocket for his wallet.

"Come on, man," says the guy with the goatee. "They're fifty bucks. Each. And if you know anything about these things then you know it's a ridiculous price."

"Not gonna argue with you there," says Grant, opening his wallet and thumbing through the bills tucked inside. "But I can see that you got a whole cart full of the things. And it looks like I'm the only one showing any interest in purchasing any of them. I got a fifty dollar bill right here..." He pulls one out of his wallet, shows it to the guy. "And it's yours in exchange for two of the masks. Take it or leave it."

The guy curses then reaches out and snatches the bill from Grant's fingers. "Fine. Grab two of them. I can't stand here haggling all day."

Grant reaches into the cart, pulls out two of the black, rubber masks, tosses one your way. "It's been a pleasure doin' business with you," he tells the goateed fellow.

"Yeah, yeah," says the other man. "Piss off now."

Grant laughs at this–he seems to find humor in any number of strange situations–and the two of you continue along your way.

"Why did you buy these things?" you ask him.

He shrugs. "Never hurts to be too prepared, now does it?"

You suppose not. Although you certainly hope that a situation does not arise in which the masks will be needed.

"Next block, and we'll hang a right," you say.

There are more flashing lights there and some police officers can actually be seen directing traffic as best they can. Across the street to your left a shout goes up. There are gunshots. *Crack! Crack!* People scatter. More gunshots. You lower your head and hurry along.

"Zombie alert!" says Grant, making a whooping siren noise. "Zombie alert!"

You reach the intersection, indicate to Grant that he should turn right.

"Good afternoon, officer," he says to the policeman standing nearby, dressed in full riot gear with a shotgun in his gloved hands. Looking out into the intersection, you see cops on every corner and two others in the middle of the street stopping and waving cars on by. The nearby officer says nothing, shows no sign that he is aware in the slightest of Grant's greeting. As you head north along the sidewalk the foot traffic almost dies out completely. It seems that the bulk of it is heading along the eastbound streets.

Halfway up to the next nonfunctioning traffic light, Grant stops and says, "Now would you look at that."

When you see what has caught his attention, you let out an exasperated sigh. "We don't have time for that," you say.

"Sure we do," he replies. "And don't tell me you can't use a little refresher."

You suppose you could. But that's not the point. Time is of the essence. The city is in a bad way and you're pretty certain that things are going to get worse before they get any better. Leaving town as quickly as possible is undoubtedly the wisest course of action. But Grant is already approaching the arched, wooden doorway with the "Open" sign hanging from its black handle and the tiny, grated window set into it at eye level. The sign swinging slightly in the breeze above the door reads "Jack's Place." The dark windows to either side of the door have dormant neon lights portraying the logos of a number of prominent imported beer companies.

"There's no way the place is really open," you tell Grant, a small part of you hoping that, in fact, the place *is* open. The thought of a "little refresher" does sound pretty damn good, you have to admit.

Grant grabs the handle. Pulls. The door doesn't budge. "Oh, well isn't that the pits?" he says. Then he raises his hand in a fist and beats on the door. "Come on, now, open up! I've got quite a thirst and a wallet full of cash. How about one more sale before the zombies chase your last customer away?"

"No one's there," you tell him, feeling the small disappointment at this realization quickly replaced by the constant anxiety that has dogged you since you saw the world going to hell from your apartment balcony. "Let's keep moving. No telling how long before–"

The door makes an audible clicking sound then swings open. An older, heavyset fellow, with a fringe of grey hair surrounding the bald peak of his head and what appears to be an antiquated but well kept shotgun in his hands, pointed directly into Grant's midsection, steps into the doorway from the gloom.

"And what can I do for you gentlemen?' he asks.

Grant spreads his hands out wide, shows that they are empty, that he is no threat at all.

"Sorry if we disturbed you," Grant tells the man, his voice surprisingly calm and steady to your ears, given the circumstances. "But we saw the open sign and were hopin' that we might be able to come in and buy a couple'a drinks."

"Show me some money," says the man with the shotgun.

Grant nods his head, reaches for his pocket and his wallet once again.

"Real slow now," the man tells him.

Eventually, Grant has his wallet out and he's got it open, exposing the money held within.

The shotgun lowers and now the man is grinning. "Sorry about all that. Can't be too sure of anyone at the moment. But never let it be said that Jack Holiday ever turned away a paying customer. Especially one who looks as desperate for a drink as you do."

Turn to page 90.

"I like your spirit," says Dora. She smiles. You find yourself smiling back. She leans in close to you, puts a hand on your shoulder and says in a low, confidential tone, "All right, here's the plan. I'm going to hit that door with everything I've got. It doesn't look very heavy or like it's been reinforced in any way. If I hit it right that lock's gonna give way. Then I'm gonna go through. You come right behind me. They've obviously got something in mind for us later on so I'm hoping that anyone standing guard out there's a bit reluctant to shoot us. If we're fast enough, we won't even give them the opportunity."

She slaps you lightly on the shoulder, takes a step back, does a few squats to loosen up, swings her arms about, bends forward and touches her toes. Then she straightens, breathes deeply a few times through her nose, her mouth set in a grim line of determination.

"You ready?" she asks.

"Whenever you are." You hope you sound like you mean it.

"Okay then."

With that, she bursts toward the door in an explosion of motion, brings her right knee up to her chest and launches a powerful kick, the bottom of her foot connecting with the door just to the left of the handle. There is a cracking, splintering, crunching sound and, just like that, the door swings open. That Dora is one impressive lady. Not missing a step, she rushes out through the open doorway, hands curled into fists, the muscles of her forearms rippling. Motivated by the physical display you've just witnessed, you let loose with a wordless shout and follow Dora out of the room.

The two people who led you to the room earlier are there. This wholly unexpected little maneuver has apparently taken them by surprise. It seems that they were in mid-conversation and are only now starting to bring the muzzles of their weapons up and around in your direction. Dora's fist catches one of them in the face, the sound of it like a baseball bat connecting for a homerun shot. Your attack is not nearly so fluid or precise. You simply lower your shoulder and run into the other guard. There is the sound of the back of the man's head striking the wall along the other side of the hallway, of the air rushing from his lungs, of the gun discharging. The shot is nearly deafening in the enclosed space. And then there is the pain.

A bright, blooming, mushroom cloud of pain in your left thigh, midway between hip and knee. You cry out and stumble backward, watch in shock as Dora practically seems to levitate off the ground, to whirl around in the air and deliver a vicious roundhouse kick to the side of the second guard's head.

And just like that, the melee is over.

Unfortunately for you, the pain cannot be vanquished so easily. You reach down and place a hand over the bleeding hole in your thigh. The world around you is going out of focus. It's hard to breathe. Dora's voice seems to come to you from somewhere far away.

"Shit! Can you stand?"

She has a gun in her hand. With her free hand she is pulling at your shirt, trying to get you to your feet.

"We have to move. They'll be coming for us."

Crying out, and with Dora's help, you climb to your feet. The pain is nearly overwhelming. Blood pours down your leg in a hot stream. Did the bullet hit an artery? The hallway swims in and out of focus around you. Bile rises in your throat. You swallow against it, trying not to vomit.

"This way," says Dora. She takes one of your arms, drapes it over her shoulder. The two of you head off down the hallway. You have no idea which direction she is leading you. There is shouting coming from somewhere behind you, the words indecipherable. Then something you can understand:

"Stop! Now! Or we'll shoot!"

Dora spins the two of you around, facing back in the direction from which you have fled.

"Eat shit!" she yells, lifts her gun hand, and fires off three quick shots.

Then she's turning you around again, continuing to flee down the hallway.

"In here," she says. You see that you are being led toward an open doorway. Light streams out of it into the dim hallway. That's when you hear the *pop-pop-pop!* of gunfire from behind you. And then you're falling to the floor. There's no pain, though. No *new* pain, that is. You haven't been hit a second time. But you're lying on the floor all the same. *Dora?* you wonder, turning your head to look at her. She's lying beside you, staring back at you. Staring but not seeing. Wide eyes glazed, unblinking, blood flowing down the side of her face.

Oh, Jesus.

The sound of footsteps approaching.

"The prophet will not be happy," you hear someone say.

"Not like we had much of a choice," says another voice. Distant. So distant now. Just on the edge of hearing.

A warm wetness underneath you. Have you pissed yourself? No. You remember the blood pouring out of you. It's getting harder to breathe. The world around you is going dark. Dora's eyes, her face, fading away, fading to grey and then black.

The sound of your heartbeat, impossibly loud in your ears.

Thump-thump.

Thump-thump.

The cold, setting in.

The quiet.

Thump...

And then nothing at all.

THE END

You turn left. The railing and the dark waters of the river beyond are to your right. You're trying to remember geography of the area. It's just not a section of town you travel in all that often, especially on foot. But you're pretty certain that you'll come to a bridge within the next mile or so. A bank of trees ahead between the road and the river obstructs your view and makes it impossible to know for sure.

Foot traffic is fairly light here and the people that you do encounter–mostly individuals, but there are a few small groups interspersed along the way–either keep their heads down or offer nothing more than a quick greeting, intent as they are on finding their own ways to safety. Cars zip by in both directions along the road here. Although you imagine they'll find the going much slower when they near the bridges or any of the other points of exit leading out of the city.

As you near the patch of trees that has been blocking your view further down the river, a man steps out of the small stretch of woodland and walks over to the railing. He looks directly at you as you approach then holds up a hand, apparently wanting you to stop. Curious, you do.

"Looking for a way out of the city?" asks the man. He is a bit short, not much more than five-and-a-half feet tall, but stocky. Wears a tight fitting T-shirt to display his muscular physique. Khaki shorts and brown hiking boots. His hair is dark and shaggy, a bit unkempt. Wide brown eyes under thick eyebrows. A nose that looks like it's been broken a time or two in the past. On his right arm between shoulder and elbow is a tattoo of a skull. And sticking out of the right front pocket of his shorts is the butt of a pistol, of course.

"Who isn't?" you respond.

"I can get you out. Right now. No waiting around at the bridges or any of the checkpoints. Places are freakin' zombie beacons." He chuckles then his face goes serious again. "I can see you thinking: Hey, who the hell is this guy? And can he really do what he says? Well, in answer to the first question: My name is Tony." He reaches his hand out toward you, obviously wanting to shake. You just stare at the hand until he lowers it. "Fair enough. You don't know me from Adam. And with the way things are going around here, I can't fault your lack of trust." He clears his throat, turns and spits on the ground before continuing. "As for the second question... I most certainly *can* do what I say. Because I've got a boat. And I am in need of one last passenger before I set off across the river. And all it will cost you, all that this life-saving little venture will set you back is a paltry one hundred dollars. Cash, of course. So what do you say? Ready to get out of this zombie hellhole? Ready to cross the river and rejoin the rest of the civilized world?"

Sure you are. But there's only one small problem.

"I don't have that much cash on me."

"Okay, then, how much you got?"

You tell him.

He seems to think about it for a moment. Then he nods his head as if coming to a decision. "Good enough. And don't let it ever be said that Tony Estrada isn't willing to help someone when they are in need. Now, let's see that money."

"Let's see the boat first."

"Ah. Very shrewd. You know how to handle your business. Right this way then"

He turns and starts to walk back into the trees.

If you decide that this all sounds a bit too shady, turn to page 112.

If you take Tony up on his offer, turn to page 182

"Damn it," you curse under your breath. Then, louder: "Grant?" No answer. "Grant!" Still silence from the convenience store. "I'm coming in!"

You make your way in through the open doorway with the handgun held out before you. The power is out here, too, and the interior of the place is dim. There's still plenty of light, however, to see that the place has been thoroughly ransacked. A couple of shelves have been toppled. Magazines litter the floor as do empty candy boxes and beer and soda cans. A short distance away, like an island near the center of the small establishment, is the rectangular service counter atop which rests a broken cash register, an empty chewing gum display, and a hat rack now devoid of the various baseball caps it once displayed. Grant is standing at the opening that leads into the island, hands hanging at his sides, head bowed as if he is transfixed by something on the floor.

"Grant?

No response. He doesn't even look at you.

"What is it?"

As you walk up behind him you hear it, a wet ripping and smacking sound, like that made by an animal at a particularly prized meal. You look over his shoulder to see what has transfixed him so. And immediately wish that you hadn't.

The dead body of a man, dressed in the red vest of a store employee, lies face down on the black and white checkered linoleum of the floor there. Sitting next to the body is a young boy, maybe ten or eleven years old at the most. Or what used to be a young boy. Because, it is obvious that the kid is no longer human. He stares up at you and Grant with milky white eyes. His skin is pale and mottled, apparent even in the room's wan lighting. In his hands the child -thing holds the arm of the corpse lying next to him. And as you watch, the zombie buries its teeth into the meaty portion of the lower arm, just below the elbow, yanks a piece of muscle away and chews deliberately, mouth open, before swallowing the morsel. The boy's chin and cheeks are smeared with gore. You can feel the alcohol you drank earlier threatening to rise up and into your throat.
Now it's your turn to say it: "Oh, Jesus."

Before you realize what's happening, before you can do anything to stop it—would you have stopped it anyway?—Grant raises his right arm, points the barrel of the handgun he carries at the undead creature before him, and pulls the trigger. Thankfully, you were able to close your eyes just in time.

Moments later, you are outside, bent over, hands on your knees, taking in deep breaths of the warm evening air. It isn't long before Grant walks out of the store and stands beside you. There is the flick of a lighter; you smell a waft of cigarette smoke.

"Nice of them to leave a pack behind," says Grant. His voice is flat, hollow sounding. The two of you stand there for a minute. The nausea that threatened to overwhelm you starts to subside.

"You all right?" asks Grant.

"Yeah, I'm fine. You?"

He takes a long drag off his cigarette, nods his head. "Smoke?" He offers the pack of cigarettes to you.

"No thanks."

He puts the pack and the lighter in a pocket of his pants.

"Okay, then. Let's go."

Turn to page 118.

Jack deadbolts the sturdy wooden door behind you. Hard to imagine any zombies forcing their way in past such a formidable obstacle. The windows, on the other hand, have you a bit concerned.

"Not to worry," says Jack, catching the direction of your gaze. "Been watching the dumb, dead SOB's wandering back and forth all morning now. Too dark for them to see in, I guess. And if they can't see you, seems they don't have much interest in you. Like you don't even exist at all. Reminds me of that creature in the *Hitchhiker's Guide to the Galaxy.* You ever read it?"

You and Grant both tell him that, sorry, no you haven't.

"That's too bad. Damn good book. Funny as all get out. Was sorry when the guy who wrote it died."

By this point, Jack has made his way across the room and behind the bar that runs the length of the wall there. A row of taps is set up near the left end of the bar itself. Behind it, and along the wall, are rows of shelves holding bottles of every type and description of alcohol imaginable. Directly in the center of the wall, between all those glorious rows of bottles, is an open doorway leading into another room beyond. Before the bar stands a dozen or so stools. Some wooden tables and chairs are placed seemingly at random about the room. The game and the jukebox are both turned off but the dimly glowing lights over the bar offer evidence that the place has electricity.

"So you've got power here?" asks Grant as a way of opening a conversation.

"Power's still out but I've got a generator up on the roof. Gives me enough juice to keep the beer cold and the ice from melting. You know, in case of an emergency." He nods his head toward the front door, laughs a little. "So what will you fellas be drinking today?"

The sight of those silver taps sweating in the slightly less than balmy air looks too enticing for you to pass up.

"A beer sounds good," you say.

"Domestic? Import?" The big man pulls a glass out of an electric cooler behind the bar and makes his way over to the taps.

"I think a Guinness would hit the spot."

"One Guinness, coming up."

"And I'll have a Jim Beam and Coke," says Grant.

"Sure thing."

A minute later, you and Grant are enjoying your drinks. Your beer tastes thick and cold and perfect in the warm room.

You spot a portable radio sitting on one of the shelves behind the bar. "Any news?" you ask.

"Nah. Pretty much the same thing all day. That's why I turned it off." Jack turns and looks at the radio. "I can turn it back on if you want."

"If you don't mind," you tell him. "Never know when there might be breaking news."

You set your beer next to where you placed your gas mask on the bar, lean forward and listen to what the announcer on the radio has to say. Whatever station Jack found seems to be a fairly informative one as the woman's voice issuing from the speaker says that there are new developments regarding the source of the dark, drifting gas that started the whole ordeal.

"*The building from which* the stain—*as people have taken to calling it—has issued is apparently registered to a rather prominent pharmaceutical company. Until we have attained more evidence, we will, for the time being, refrain from disclosing the company's name...*"

"Yeah, don't want to mess with any of the pharmaceutical companies," says Jack. "Accuse one of them incorrectly and you'll have your ass sued off."

"*Simple inhalation of the gas seems to be sufficient in turning a perfectly healthy individual into one of these... zombies. Yes, it will kill you. Reports estimate that within an hour of inhaling the stuff you will die. Very unpleasantly. And then it will bring you—somehow... some way—back to life. Or some semblance of life.* Un-*life may be a more accurate term, for as the zombie gives off the appearance of still being alive in some way... That it is still capable of getting up and walking around... From what I'm being told, it has no pulse nor does it need to breathe. Apparently, it only needs to devour the flesh of the living to fuel whatever strange energy fills its undead body. Most theories center around a virus of some kind. A* manmade *virus of some kind. Developed in a lab within the building where the leak occurred. For what reason is anybody's guess. Although most of our callers seem to agree that the government has something to do with it, that the gas would undoubtedly serve some sort of military purpose..."*

Jack turns off the radio. "Well, no shit," he says. "Anyone need another drink?"

"No, I'm good," you say. The beer before you is still more than half full.

"I'll have another," says Grant. You give him a look. He smiles. "I'm buyin'. Go ahead and drink up." Probably not the best idea you've ever heard. Need to keep your wits about you if you're going to see your way through this thing. One beer. That's it. Then it's time to move on. With or without Grant. Delay too long and you might never be able to get out of here.

"How come you haven't left?" you ask Jack and take another sip of beer.

"You mean why haven't I fled the city like most sensible folks have?"

You nod.

"I've been here for twenty-six years. Survived two recessions. Back in eighty-two this place nearly burned to the ground. Spent three months gutting and rebuilding it. Let's see... Two years after that there was a shooting. Three people were killed. Right over there by the pool table. Some gang related thing, apparently... A few years back a guy lost control of his car, plowed right through the front of the building. Luckily, it was early in the morning. Nobody here. I was upstairs sleeping. That's a hell of a way to be woken up, let me tell you. Shut me down for nearly two months that time. I've been audited by the IRS twice. Offered buyouts more times than I can remember. Proposed to my wife—God rest her soul—less than a month after I opened the joint. Got down on one knee right there in the middle of the floor and asked if she would marry me. It was a busy night. All those people watching to see if I'd just made a complete ass of myself." He chuckles. "Luckily, I didn't. We were married for nearly thirteen years. Then the cancer got her. Drank myself into the worst stupor of my life sitting where you are now the night she died." He sighed, reached into the cooler and pulled out a bottle of Budweiser, popped the cap and took a long pull. "Hell, I got half my life tied up in this place. So if you think I'm gonna let a bunch of walking dead pieces of–"

A loud crashing noise interrupts this little soliloquy. Startled, you drop your glass of beer–or what's left of it. It falls to the floor and breaks, the sound submerged beneath the awful racket made by one of the large windows behind you shattering inward, of all that glass faling in broken shards to the floor's hard surface.

"Jesus Christ!" shouts Grant and you turn in time to see the figure of a man silhouetted in the light streaming in through the now mostly empty window frame. The only parts of the window itself that remain are ragged pieces of glass like broken teeth jutting from the edges. You blink against the sudden brightness, unable to make out the facial features of the man in the window. Before you can say anything, a most terrible sound emerges from the man, a wordless shout that rises in pitch like the howl of a wounded animal. Other figures crowd in. When the shouting dies down you can hear the collective moaning of the others that have gathered there.

"Out of the way!" you hear Jack shout from behind you. Leaping to your feet, you step to the side just as the big man grabs a shotgun from under the bar, swings the barrel up and around in the direction of the broken window, utters a most profound and colorful curse, then opens fire. The *booming* of the weapon is an assault on the ears in the enclosed space. The barman's aim is true, though, and the howler staggers back from the window. The dead ones, the true zombies, they seem completely ignorant to any potential danger the three of you represent. They continue to moan as two, three, four of them start to pull themselves over the bottom part of the window frame and into the bar.

"Oh, no you don't!" says Jack. He comes out from behind the counter, looking to get a closer shot at the invaders. *Boom!* goes the shotgun again.

"Hell, yeah, let's do this!" Grant shouts from a few feet beside you. He already has his handgun out, is firing indiscriminately into the undead crowd before you. Not wanting your new friends to have all the fun–or so you tell yourself, trying to ride an emotional wave of alcohol boosted bravado–you pull your own gun free from where it is tucked down the front of your pants, aim at the nearest zombie, and pull the trigger. The room is filled with the deafening cacophony of three guns erupting. Zombies are falling, one by one, but still they come, uncaring of the consequences of such an ill-advised advance. The shotgun discharges a couple more rounds. You and Grant are forced to reload. Another minute or so of firing ensues. You toss an empty box of cartridges to the floor. The air is thick with the odor of gunpowder and massacred zombies. Not a pleasant smell, to be sure. As you go to reload again Jack shouts, "Fall back! There's too many of them!" You turn in time to see him running back around the bar. Grant plants his hands on the wooden bar top and performs a rather admirable vault over it. You take Jack's lead and, after grabbing your gas mask from where you left it on the bar top, retreat as well.

Behind the bar, you follow the other two men through the doorway located between the bottle lined shelves. Once through, Jack pushes the door closed. This one is also wooden but not nearly as formidable as the one at the bar's entrance. Still, it should be able to hold the invading zombies at bay. At least for a little while. Especially if that initial shotgun blast was able to take the howler completely out of the picture. Maybe, maybe not. Who knows what physical reserves the mad creature is capable of calling upon? And where there's one howler there can always be more...

You find yourself in a storage room about a third the size of the establishment's main room. It is mostly filled with cases of beer stacked one on top of the other, brown boxes filled with bottles of alcohol, and a dozen or so silver kegs. There are also various boxes of cleaning supplies. Along one wall, a staircase runs up to the floor above, presumably to Jack's living quarters. A second doorway is set into the wall opposite the one through which you just fled. It probably leads out behind the bar, either onto a street there or into an alleyway.

"What now?" asks Grant. He doesn't seem all that worried. More excited than anything. Yeah, the guy's just a little bit crazy, all right. But crazy might be just what you need if you want to make it out of this place–and, hopefully, the city–with any part of your skin intact.

There comes the sound of something thumping against the wooden door that leads back out into the bar. Then, much to your despair, you hear another thumping sound from the doorway that leads out to the back of the building.

"Let's barricade the doors," says Jack. "Help me roll some of these kegs over."

"But then we'll be trapped!" says Grant, looking about a bit wild-eyed. "For all we know, that crowd out there could just keep on gettin' bigger!"

"You got a better idea?" asks Jack.

Grant raises his gun. "Yeah! Let's blast our way outta here while we still got a chance!"

"That's crazy talk," says Jack. "We need to barricade these doors then head upstairs. There's another door up there. It's gonna take them a long time to get through two sets of locked and reinforced doorways. I don't care how many of those monsters there are."

"But eventually they're *gonna* get through," Grant retorts. "And then we're screwed. I say we make a break for it. Go back out the way we came in. At least we know what's out there. Don't waste any ammo. Get up close. Nothing but headshots. We can make it." He turns toward you. "Well? How 'bout it?"

If you agree that you need to get out of there but think the back exit is the safer bet, turn to page 106.

If Grant's craziness is infectious and you decide to go along with his plan, turn to page 126.

If you like Jack's way of thinking, decide to head upstairs and wait things out, turn to page 146.

You're shaking your head, practically yelling at Dora: "No! This way! Follow me."

Then you take off after pulling at her arm.

"All right! All right!" she shouts.

Then the two of you are making your way through the fray, dodging around people, running away from the howlers.

"Hold up!" you hear Dora say from behind you, turn to see her grabbing the end of a broken two-by-four, about a foot-and-a-half in length, from one of the fires, holding it out before her like a torch. "Let me lead," she tells you and sets off into the tunnel.

You follow, the sounds of chaos chasing you into the wet darkness of the corridor.

"Gotta make this quick," says Dora. "This fire isn't gonna last long."

You reach a fork in the tunnel. Without hesitating, Dora takes the right hand branch. Does she have an idea of how to get out of here? Probably not. You don't even see a point in asking. Keep moving, that's all that matters. Put as much distance between the two of you and the howlers as you can. The sounds of their screaming echo down the tunnel, chasing you through the claustrophobic, flickering darkness. You hope some of the others managed to get away. It seems that you and Dora were the only ones to choose this tunnel as an exit. Or maybe there were others who had gone in ahead of you, had chosen to head left where Dora went right. Who knows? There's nothing you can do to help any of them. It's going to take plenty of luck for just the two of you to make it out of here alive.

You come to several more branches of the tunnel. Dora does not hesitate in her decisions. Left. Right. Left. Without pause. The light from her makeshift torch is dying. It won't be long before the two of you are immersed in total darkness. There has to be a ladder around here somewhere, you keep telling yourself, like the one that brought you down here in the first place.

The sounds of howler screaming is distant, muted. It seems that none of the monsters have come after you. For that, at least, you can be thankful. Now if only a way out would present itself.

Dora leads you out onto a rickety bridge made of grated metal panels with rusted, waist high railings to either side. It's just wide enough for one person at a time to cross. From the darkness below comes the sound of rushing water, like that of a river bloated by rainfall. The bridge is a good thirty feet across. The air is thick with the odor of raw sewage here. Dora is pounding across the span in front of you. Is it your imagination, or is the bridge swaying beneath your feet?

With a cry of surprise and a screech of metal Dora disappears from in front of you. Before you even realize what is happening, you step forward and then find yourself falling. Not far though. Almost immediately you plunge into the vile river rushing beneath the bridge. Go under deep enough to touch the bottom with your feet. Force yourself up to the surface, sputtering, retching from the filthy water that filled your mouth and forced its way down your throat. The darkness around you is absolute as you are carried along by the water's current, flailing your arms and kicking your feet in a desperate effort to keep from drowning. You slam up against one side of the corridor and then the other through which the river is rushing as it twists and turns along its subterranean course. You swallow more water, throw it back up. On and on the awful journey continues until you're convinced that you no longer have the strength to keep fighting for air.

And then there is light. Faint at first, but quickly intensifying. Ahead, you can see a great circular maw of bright white light. The literal light at the end of the tunnel. You redouble your efforts, tread the water with the last of your fading strength. A roaring sound reaches your ears and then you are cast out through that circle of light, out through the air on a fountain of what you have come to realize is chemically treated sewage. For a brief, terrifying moment you are airborne. And then you slam down into the much cleaner waters of the river that borders the south side of the city here.

You're forced down deep by the water escaping the tunnel with you. After what seems like an eternity of pulling yourself to the surface, you thrust your head up and into the sweet, outdoor air, gasping for all you're worth. Meanwhile, you manage to pull off your shoes and socks so that you might swim a little easier. After you've regained your breath somewhat, you try to relax, tread water, and get your bearings.

The current has pushed you pretty far out into the river. The nearest bank looks awfully far away. But you've always been a pretty good swimmer. You just hope you've got enough strength left to reach safety.

It dawns on you that someone is calling your name. Turning in a circle, you catch sight of an arm raised above the surface of the river a good fifty or so feet downstream, waving toward you. Recognizing the voice, you know that it's Dora. A wave of relief washes over you. You find that the sight of her helps to revive your strength a little. For the first time in what seems like a long time, you start to believe that you're actually going to make it through this alive. After all, you've nearly reached your destination. Make your way to the far bank and you're out of the city, the river a barrier between you and the zombie horde. It may not have been the most heroic of escapes but you'll take it. Alive is alive, after all. And that's all that matters.

You start to swim toward Dora.

And that's when something grabs your leg. A number of somethings, actually. You see, you're not the only thing to find yourself washed away and into the river. There's a new breed of creature inhabiting these waters. It can't swim very well but, then again, it doesn't have to. Because it doesn't even need to breathe. It can walk around on the bottom if to wants to. Push upward, see if any tasty morsel has come along. The one way that the zombies do resemble fish is the way that they travel in groups, as if by some unspoken command. Four of them have you now. Pulling you down. Biting. Clawing. The distant shore might as well be a million miles away for all the chance you ever have of reaching it.

THE END

You turn right. The road makes a gradual curve to the northwest. Follow it far enough and you'll end up in the heart of the business district, over by the stadium. Over by where the lab exploded and released the gas that brought the zombies to your city. Probably not a good idea to head off too far in that direction. If you don't come to a bridge that will take you across the river within a half dozen blocks or so, you tell yourself, you're going to turn around and head back in the other direction.

The sound of something screaming reaches you from somewhere off to your right, back in the direction from which you have just fled. It is a terrible, animalistic sound, like something being slowly tortured to death, or trapped with no hope of escape, or filled with some awful, inescapable urge to kill and destroy. You have no doubt that it is one of the howlers that you heard about making the sound. You stop for a second, legs momentarily going stiff with dread. The sound comes again, slightly louder now, like thunder before an approaching storm. The thought of the thing making that hideous noise coming your way spurs your legs into action once again. You walk and then break into a mild jog as you continue along the sidewalk between the roadway and the black metal railing. To your right is the city and enough monsters to fill a thousand childhood nightmares. To your left, the river. And ahead? Hopefully some way to cross that river and leave those legions of the walking dead behind.

A car passes by along the road to your right. Another one. Two more in quick succession. None of them stop and you do nothing to try and make them pull over. The encounter with the masked man has left you shaken. You have no wish to meet another monster of the living variety.

You reach a point where you can see the bridge ahead spanning the river out to your left. At two points along the bridge's length, silver towers rise about thirty feet into the air, the foundations disappearing beneath the bridge into the waters below. The thick, silver main cables form a sort of upside down W and are connected to the bridge itself by dozens of vertically running suspension cables. The sight of the thing, the promise of escape it offers, fills you with relief and no small amount of happiness. You've made it. On your own. You're a survivor. Soon, you'll be on the other side of the river. And you won't stop there. You'll keep moving away from the city. Find somewhere to rent a car. You've got your wallet, your debit and credit cards. With any luck, you'll be spending the night a hundred miles from here, watching reports of the zombie infestation on a TV screen in the comfort of a hotel room.

The way forward begins to slow as you near the bridge. Vehicle traffic comes to a complete stop a good quarter mile from the entrance to the bridge. Foot traffic grows increasingly thick the nearer the bridge you get, eventually coalesces into a crowd which you have to push your way through in order to reach the point where the sidewalk merges with the bridge itself. Staying close to the railing, you step out onto the bridge. From this new vantage point, you can see the sloping ground below and the river's edge. You move along slowly for a minute or so and then find that you cannot take another step forward. People are packed one against the other. The sounds of murmuring, angry rumblings and whimpering children reach you from all sides. The air is thick with exhaust fumes from the cars and trucks idling nearby. No one is sure why traffic has ground to a halt like this, judging by the conversations of those around you. Rumor has it that some branch of the military–army, more than likely, one guy says–has set up a check point on the other bank, is making sure that no one has been bitten, is carrying the virus–or whatever it is that causes one to turn into the living dead–out of the city. The crowd inches forward. Inches forward again. You pull out your cell phone, check for signal, try to dial a random number stored within its memory. No luck. The network is, undoubtedly, still overloaded. And that isn't likely to change any time soon.

You overhear snatches of conversation, people relating harrowing tales of escape. And then, from behind you, the sound of screaming can be heard. More like a screeching, actually. So full of hurt, and confusion, and insanity. You are sweating from the afternoon heat and the close proximity of so many other bodies, but suddenly you feel yourself go cold all over. That scream... It comes again and is joined by others. You get the impression that there are at least four or five different creatures making the sounds. Loud.

Like they could be nearing the rear edge of the crowd within mere moments.

The crowd surges forward, packing itself even tighter into the space available. You can *sense* the panic in those pressing up behind you, the feeling flowing into you too. More screaming. Frightened shouts. Crying. Something gives in the crowd ahead of you and everyone lunges forward. A step. Two. Then it is like the proverbial floodgates have opened and people are walking, struggling forward, pushing at one another, trying to find room to flee.

"Oh, God, no. No!" someone screams from not very far behind you. People are starting to go over the railing onto the main part of the bridge where the cars are idling. And then there is room ahead of you, not much, but enough to let you break into a sort of dodging run, enough to make your way past those slower than yourself. Enough space to flee.

And flee you do, fear and panic fueling your strides. *Got to get away*, you tell yourself over and over. And then you fall. Something has tripped you. You're not sure what. But you go down hard, only just manage to get your hands down in time to take some of the impact. The air *whooshes* from your lungs as you hit the ground, face down. Someone steps on your back. Another person. Further pushing the air from your body. And then people are trampling you, heedless of your plight. You feel something crack midway up your spine. Feel ribs gives way. On and on it goes, a relentless pounding. A boot slams down on the outstretch fingers of your left hand, smashing them. Then someone stomps you on the back of the head, hard, and you know no more.

Hey, at least the zombies didn't get you. Not while you were conscious, anyway. Good to see that there's always a bright side, isn't it?

THE END

"Grant!" you shout from where you stand on the sidewalk. What the hell has he gotten himself into in there? You call out again. No answer. Should you go in after him? If the roles were reversed, you know that he would. Yeah, he's a bit crazy though, isn't he? At least, that's the vibe you've been getting from him since the moment you two met. No sense letting his rash behavior get the both of you in trouble. No, you're going to stay right where you are. If he needs your help, he can damn well ask for it. And what if he does ask? Do you go into the store then?

The loud *bang!* of a gunshot emanates from the store's entrance, startling you. What's going on in there? Nothing good, obviously. Maybe the guy really does need your help. Maybe he's just too proud—or too nuts—to ask. Or maybe now he can't ask.

"Grant?"

No answer.

"Shit."

You snap open the cylinder of the .38 Special in your hand, double check to make sure it's still got some rounds in it. Can never be too certain in a situation like this, you tell yourself. Or are you just stalling? Satisfied that the gun will work properly when you need it to, you close the cylinder, take a deep breath, and step toward the open doorway of the convenience store.

Just as Grant steps out from the gloomy interior beyond. He's fishing a cigarette out of the pack he's carrying. With a shaking hand he puts the cigarette to his mouth, lights it with the lighter he must have found inside too. Then he takes a deep drag of the cigarette, holds it for a few moments, lets out a cloud of smoke with a deep sigh.

"What the hell happened in there?"

He just stares at you, like he's trying to figure out who you are. That look worries you, to put it mildly. Then it's like something has clicked in his mind and he blinks, offers a little smile, holds the pack of cigarettes out to you.

"Interest you in a smoke?"

"Ummm... No thanks."

"Nice of the thievin' bastards ta leave *somethin'* behind." His accent seems more pronounced than usual.

He puts the pack and the lighter in a pocket of his jeans, looks off in the direction the two of you were headed before his little detour.

"Shall we continue then?" Without waiting for a response, he walks away. You think about grabbing him by the arm and asking him again about what happened inside the store then think better of it. If he wants you to know, he'll tell you, when he's good and ready. And maybe, in the end, it's something you're better off not knowing about. With a sigh of your own you head off after him.

Turn to page 118.

"Yes, we need to keep moving," you say. Grant nods his head vigorously in agreement. A scowl crosses Jack's face. "And you're right, we don't know what's in store for us out front. Let's check the back first. It may be safer out there."

"Fine, fine," says Grant and he walks over to the back door. There is a deadbolt which he disengages. Jack lowers his shotgun, aims it toward the door, backs away. Grant looks back over his shoulder at you.

"Go ahead," you tell him. "Just a crack. Any sign of trouble then slam it closed."

"Or get the hell out of the way," says Jack, motioning with the shotgun.

Grant pulls on the handle, opens the door an inch, maybe two. He puts his eye to the opening, peers through to the alley beyond. Then he pushes it closed, turns and leans with his back against it.

"Good call," he says. "Practically deserted out there. I could only see two of the rotting things wandering about. You ready to do this?"

"Damn straight," you say. Walking over to Jack, you hold out your hand, tell him how much you've appreciated the hospitality. He takes your hand, gives it a firm shake. "Anytime. When all of this blows over, make sure you stop on by again."

"Will do." With that you walk over to where Grant is waiting. You snap open the .38, make sure it's fully loaded. Then you look Grant in the eye, give a nod toward the door and say, "All right. Let's do it."

He stands away from the door, turns and pulls it open. No zombies come bursting in. He steps out into the alleyway beyond. You follow a few feet behind him.

"Good luck and God speed!" Jack calls out before closing and locking the door.

The alley is maybe fifteen feet across. To your right it dead ends at a two story brick wall. To the left it opens out onto the street beyond, about forty feet away. A few doors are set into the walls along either side of the alleyway. Almost directly before you stands a yellow, metal Dumpster against the wall opposite Jack's place. No, the alley is not very wide but the few zombies present are slow–as they all tend to be–and rather easily avoided. No sense in gunning them down for no reason. Best to save your ammo for when it might really be needed. Grant agrees. And so the two of you start off at a jog, maneuvering around the walking corpses and making good time toward the mouth of the alley.

As you approach the street beyond, you see a couple of cars go by, both of them headed toward the east. You see some people, too, moving in small groups. One group walks briskly by. The one that follows has broken into an all out run.

"Might be trouble," says Grant, slowing down a bit, letting you get up next to him. Side by side–you to the left, Grant to the right–the two of you exit the alleyway.

As soon as you step past the corner formed by the building there, something bumps into you, knocking you a step to your right, almost into Grant. Then that something is grabbing you, pulling at your shirt, leaning its face in toward you like it might want to kiss you. But instead, it opens its mouth wide and howls. The breath that washes over you is foul enough to make you wince, to cause your eyes to water. It's a woman that has you, slightly overweight, hair pulled up in a loose bun on top of her head, strands dangling down across a face sporting two black eyes and a bleeding, crooked nose. Her eyes are wide, darting back and forth wildly. She keeps pulling at you, nearly causing you to lose your balance completely and tumble to the pavement. You try to bring your gun up but she's in too close so you jam the barrel into her abdomen and pull the trigger. The screaming cuts off almost abruptly. She stumbles back a step, pulling you with her. Then the howler coughs, sending spittle into your face. You fire again but still she does not release her grip. All the while Grant is behind you yelling, "Shit! Shit! Shit!" The woman leans in again and breathes out, directly into your face. And this breath is even worse than what you have just experienced. For one, it comes out dark, like a big puff of burning oil smoke. And it burns. Suddenly, your eyes are watering in earnest and you're forced to close them. Without meaning to, you pull in a breath of your own, sucking the vile, dark air into your mouth, down your throat, and into your lungs, all of which starts to burn like it's been spritzed with acid. Only then does the howler release its grip on you, turn and start to run away.

Grant takes a few steps after the woman, firing twice in her direction. Whether he was able to hit her or not you can't tell as you are effectively blinded, and the burning sensation now flooding your respiratory system is a terrible thing commanding all of your attention.

You can't breathe and your legs feel weak, so weak that you find it easier to fall to the ground. The pain is overwhelming, seeming to spread outward and into every area of your body. You start to cough, hacking violent coughs, each of which feels as though it must surely tear the lining from your esophagus. The world is washed away in a blinding red wave of agony. And for a time, you know nothing else.

Until...

You climb to your feet. The pain has subsided to a dull, persistent ache. It tingles along the countless nerve endings throughout the whole of your being, leaving you incapable of any form of rational thought. The pain is everything. Your world. Your master. And as your master it commands you to move. To find others to whom you can offer the pain. To pass it along as a gift. A most unappreciated gift, to be sure, but a gift nonetheless. You look around, trying to find Grant. But he is gone. Your rapidly darting eyes cannot see him anywhere. Then comes the rage. Nearly as all-consuming as the ache gripping your mind and body. You open your mouth wide and scream. No, you *howl*. An animalistic expression of all the ugly, terrible feelings swirling about within you. The pain commands you to move again. And so you do. There are people across the street, frightened people who see you and start to run away. You run after them. Out into the street. But, unfortunately, it seems that you've forgotten the old adage about looking both ways, the one your mother taught you when you were a child. The car slams on the brakes but not in time to keep from striking you with its right front bumper. Something cracks in your hip and you are thrown a good ten feet through the air before coming down and skidding across the pavement, tearing chunks of skin away from the exposed flesh of your arms. The pain is bad but it is still a lesser thing than the one that forces you to your feet, to continue the hunt, fractured hip or not, to give chase as best you can. To *howl*...

Four others you manage to infect. And now the pain is subsiding. *Everything* is subsiding. The light coming into your eyes. The sounds assaulting your ears. The need to give chase. The urge to howl.

Whimpering, you sit down, back pressed to the wall of a building. Your eyesight fades... fades... as does the pain. Your breathing slows, comes at longer and longer intervals, in more shallow and elongated inhalations. Until you stop breathing altogether. Then you fall over onto your side, lying there on the sidewalk, next to the building. And there you die. Darkness falls over you like a shroud.

For a little while, at least.

The world comes back to you. Slowly. Distant. Muted. You force yourself back into a sitting position, look around. You are sitting at the side of a road. There is a parked car before you. The sound of screaming reaches your ears. Again, distant and muted. Everything you see is tinged with red. You are hungry. So hungry. The emptiness inside of you a demanding, physical thing. It is all that matters, the satiating of this hunger. You moan.

It seems a colossal effort, climbing to your feet. But once there, you feel the world grow firm and steady beneath you. A slow and deliberate strength seems to fill your limbs. Tentatively, like something newborn, you place one foot out in front of the other. Repeat the process. A song from an old Christmas television special flits through what remains of your consciousness, a hardly remembered thing. And then it is gone and only the hunger remains.

You walk. You moan. You find others like yourself. Eventually, your group happens upon a stalled car. There are people inside the car. Living people. Living *flesh.* These people, inside that car, they're like the soft meat found within a turtle's shell. The hunger cries out. You moan. All of you moan. And then you are at the car. A convertible with a cloth roof. You tear off most of your fingernails trying to get in. Eventually, with the help of your friends, you do get in. The people, screaming for all they're worth, are dragged from the car. You give in to the hunger, submerge yourself in the sweet taste of living flesh. The thick, salty flavor of the blood, like a delicious gravy. The way the muscle comes apart in strings between your teeth. The screaming, like the sweetest of melodies...

Satiated, you drop the unmoving, mutilated thing in your hands to the ground beside the car. Again, you walk. Again, you moan. The hunger is quiet, sedated. For a time, that is. Not very long, though. No, not very long at all...

Inside someone's house, through the shattered glass of the front door.

"Stay back, God damn you! Stay back!"

Three people standing before you. All that tasty, warm, wonderful meat. You moan, reach out toward the object–no, objects–of your desire. The rifle that the man is holding discharges its deadly round. The bullet punches you in the chest, exits out your back just below the right shoulder blade. Almost enough to make you fall down. Almost. The next bullet hits you in the face, rips away a rather large chunk of your left cheek, shatters teeth and a section of bone. The damage doesn't concern you. Still plenty of teeth left with which to bite and tear and chew, with which to feed. You move forward.

The next bullet snaps your head back. And, finally, your little zombie rampage is brought to an end.

THE END

As soon as the guy wanders off into the trees you take off at a run in the direction you were headed. For all you know he's got a gang of cutthroats or some similar, unsavory characters waiting to jump and rob anyone stupid enough to follow him away from the road. You most definitely were not born yesterday. Let good ol' Tony find someone else to play his little game with.

After a minute or so of running you slow to a walk again, not wanting to tire yourself out unnecessarily or work up too great of a thirst. Who knows if you're going to have to run in earnest from an even greater threat sometime in the near future? The city has become a haven of unforeseeable threats, after all, and it would undoubtedly be in your best interest to keep that in mind and try to stay as prepared as possible for any eventuality.

You fall in behind a group of three people walking just ahead of you. To your left, the street supports an intermittent stream of automobile traffic. People are walking along the far side of the road, too. In the near distance, you can see more people walking ahead of the group before you. You assume everyone's got the same destination in mind that you do. Everyone's heading for the next bridge to take them out of here.

The sound of something exploding comes from the city, most of which sprawls away to your left. There is gunfire, distant, but disconcerting nonetheless. And there is screaming. Howling. The monsters that have overrun the city, it seems they never rest.

Looking in that direction, you are surprised when you return your attention to the sidewalk before you and see that the small group of people that you've been following has stopped moving, has turned around and is facing your way. The members of this group are young, in their early twenties, maybe late teens judging by the looks of them. Two girls and a guy. Something about them gives you the impression that they are college students. Probably out-of-towners living here for the opportunity to attend one of the city's illustrious institutes of higher learning. Right place, maybe. But definitely the wrong time.

You stop a few steps before the group, wondering what they could want.

"Do you have a gun?" asks one of the girls. She's rather plain looking, not nearly as pretty as the other one, her nose just slightly too big for her face, her eyes just a bit too close together.

"Why do you want to know?" you ask, not exactly sure how to respond to a question like that. It's not the type of thing you normally get asked. In fact, it's the first time the question has ever been addressed to you. *Just a sign of the times...*

"Because... well... we don't have one. And we thought that, if you had one..."

"We'd feel safer if you were with us," says the guy, finishing her thought. "If you have a gun, that is."

You nod your head, seeing the logic of it. "Maybe I do," you reply. "But how do you know I'm not some sort of crazy person?"

The other girl, the prettier one, speaks up for the first time: "I guess you gotta trust someone, you know?"

You process this response for a moment.

"I used to have one," you tell them, deciding to respond with the honesty that the three of them have showed you. "But it was... taken from me."

"Oh," says the first girl. The three friends exchange glances. They look your way again.

"Well, I guess you can come with us anyway," says the guy. "If you want. Safety in numbers and all that."

You smile, trying to look reassuring. "Sure, safety in numbers."

It turns out that your intuition was correct, that the three are, in fact, college students. The first girl who spoke to you, her name is Angie. The other girl is Sue. The guy is Ben. They're heading for the bridge too, which has come into view now that the line of trees near the river has all but faded away. It isn't far. Another five minutes of walking and you should be there. Even still, you're grateful for the company.

The three students joke about the fact that it looks like they're going to get some time off from school. "Unless I want to change my major to zombie studies, or something like that," says Ben.

"Zombie lit," says Angie and she giggles.

"Zombie arts and crafts," chimes in Sue.

The four of you pass a barricade off to your left, a low, portable cement wall that has been placed at the end of the street intersecting the one you've been following. There are three police officers behind the barricade wearing full body armor, standing on this side of the wall, their backs to you, rifles raised to their shoulders, sighting out and along the road before them.

"Never thought I'd be so glad to see the cops," say Ben.

One of the officers fires his rifle. The other two pop off a couple of shots of their own. They do it somewhat nonchalantly, as though they are not too concerned by whatever it is they are firing at. However, the gunfire prompts the four of you to quicken your step a bit.

Before long, your little group finds itself in a flow of thickening foot traffic. The closer you get to the bridge, the denser the growing crowd of people around you becomes. Near the entrance to the bridge, pedestrian and vehicle traffic slows to a snail's pace. Impatient drivers randomly beep their horns. Angry and concerned grumbling comes from all directions.

"No doubt, the military is controlling the flow of traffic out of the city," says Ben. "Our always efficient government officials at work."

You're thinking how this would be a terrible time for a group of howlers or a horde of the walking dead to show up. Hopefully there is enough police presence in the area to prevent such a disaster from happening.

The minutes drag by but eventually you and your newfound companions find yourselves stepping out onto the bridge. The river is wide here. Your best guess is that it has to be close to a mile across. At this pace, it will take you hours to reach the other side.

"Hopefully it clears up somewhere ahead," you say.

Time passes. Slowly. As does your progress. You are pressed up close to the bridge's guardrail and try to distract yourself with the view of the land sloping away to the water below. This only serves as entertainment for so long, however. Eventually, you move out over the river itself. Foot by torturous foot, you make your way across the bridge. The occasional boat passes by below. You and your friends have stopped conversing for some time now. The mood surrounding you is a dark one. There really isn't a whole lot to say.

Twenty minutes into the journey you hear it. The howling. It comes from somewhere behind you. Panicked shouting goes up from those gathered and crammed onto the bridge's walkways behind you. And then the crowd tries to surge forward.

People press up behind you, forcing you, in turn, into the people gathered before you. You try to flow with it as best you can but it's hard as your feet keep threatening to become entangled with those of the people around you. At some point, Sue falls down with a cry. Ben is shouting her name from right beside you. Trying to turn in that direction, you look for the fallen girl but it's hopeless. The mass of people surrounding you is too thick, too immobilizing. It's getting more and more difficult to breathe. A sense of real panic is starting to set in.

Then, thankfully, mercifully, the wall of people before you moves forward. There is room. Something at the front of the crowd has apparently given way. Concentrating on keeping your footing, you push forward, find yourself with some walking room.

"Ben? Sue? Angie?" you cry out. There is a response from somewhere behind you. There is also the terrible sound of the howler's call. And an audible chorus of moaning. The people before you and around you start to run. Not wanting to be trampled or find yourself within reach of the monsters somewhere behind you, you start to run too. Looking out over the water you're surprised to discover that you're now nearly halfway across the bridge. Just then, a cry goes up from those around you. People are pointing and shouting as they run. You nearly trip over a body lying prone on the walkway, not moving, somehow manage to keep your feet and not get trampled by those following you. Looking to your right again, in the direction which everyone is pointing, you see what has caught everyone's attention. Three airplanes are coming in, low, over the river, directly toward the bridge. Military fighters, from what you can tell at this distance. They come in quickly, growing in your field of vision like avenging angels sent to carry out God's wrath. A rather fitting image as the jet fighters release a salvo of missiles toward the section of the bridge directly before you. The jets gain altitude as they pass by overhead with a nearly deafening roar. Then the explosion rocks the walkway beneath your feet, tosses you up into the air rather effortlessly. The bridge buckles up to meet your descent, painfully slamming into your feet and crumpling your legs. You fall forward onto somebody who has collapsed in front of you. Somebody falls down on top of you. There is pain in one of your ankles, enough to convince you that it is broken. But the pain is nothing next to the terror conjured by the grinding, squealing, colossal moaning of the bridge as it lurches and collapses at its center point down into the dark and dreary currents of the river below. The surface beneath you pitches forward and you start to slide. Then more of the bridge gives way and you fall, as does everyone around you, toward the river. A great chorus of screaming joins the wounded protesting of the bridge. The drop is more than thirty feet, the surface of the water hard and unforgiving. The effect is like being slammed face first into a brick wall. The impact knocks you unconscious. A blessing, really, as you don't suffer at all while you sink and then drown beneath the dark, grasping waters of the river.

THE END

It isn't long before you approach another intersection. More blinking traffic lights. More stalled and wrecked cars. And you thought people drove like idiots when it rained around here. That sort of driving seems like the work of professionals compared to what's gone down since the dead started to walk.

To your right, on the southwestern corner of the intersection, stands a looming bank building with a wide stone staircase leading up to an entrance flanked by a pair of stone lions. And from around the far side of the bank comes a pair of men dressed in military fatigues, rifles held in their hands, running for all they are worth. They turn and come toward you, go by without stopping, slow down enough for one of them to yell, "Run! For the love of God, run!"

"So what do you think's got 'em so spooked?" asks Grant.

Then you hear it. A great moaning sound. And screaming. An utterly demented sound you've heard before, outside the entrance to your apartment building. A howler. Possibly more than one. All of a sudden it's pretty obvious what's got them so spooked.

"I think we should do what they say," you tell Grant.

"I think I agree with you."

The two of you turn and head back in the direction from which you've just come. The soldiers are already nearing the convenience store. The fear motivating their strides suddenly fills you as the moaning and the shrieking becomes a veritable wall of sound. Glancing back over your shoulder you see a thick mass of the undead come around the bank building. You break into a run only to pull up short as you see more zombies pour into the intersection ahead. With grim fascination, you watch as the soldiers stop and aim their weapons at the monsters that are all too quickly upon them. To their credit, the two men put up a descent fight, manage to fire off a couple of shots before they are surrounded and dragged under. Their screams do not last long. The moaning of the dead echoes between the buildings that line either side of the street you're on.

Grant grabs you by the arm, pulls you between a couple of cars and out into the roadway, leads you over toward the mouth of an alleyway that runs between two small apartment buildings only three stories high. A *dead end* alleyway you quickly realize.

"Hope there's a fire escape ladder or something else to climb," Grant shouts back at you as he runs.

And, yes, there are fire escapes here but the ladders are pulled up, the lower sections well out of reach. At the end of the alleyway, pressed up against the plain brick, three story wall where the two apartment buildings come together, is a yellow Dumpster. Without thinking, the two of you run toward the Dumpster, pull yourselves up and onto its closed metal lid, look about frantically for anything to climb, anything to take you upward and away from the approaching mass of zombies spilling into the alleyway behind you. But there is nothing, only a nondescript brick wall. No windows. Not even any cracks large enough to be used as finger holds.

"Shit!" says Grant, breathing rapidly.

You turn and look back toward the approaching zombies, at the pair up front that move differently from the others, much more fluidly and naturally, just like the one who escaped the wrath of your Uzi in front of the entrance of the building where you live. One of the pair screeches, a piercing, terrible sound, that reverberates in the closed confines of the alleyway. A moment later, the other one does the same. One of them is missing an arm. A woman, with half of her face and most of her long, dark hair burned away. The other one is male, dressed only in a ragged pair of dress slacks. There are long, open wounds crisscrossing his torso. They look terribly painful but the man seems to pay them no mind whatsoever. He screams and comes closer as does the mass of zombies behind him, their own voices raised in a chorus of moaning.

The howlers can't be more than twenty feet away. Fifteen... Ten... You look at Grant, see that all the bravado is gone from the look he returns. There is nothing but terror there.

"Guess this is it then," he manages to say. He reaches into the front pocket of his jeans, apparently trying to get in one last cigarette.

Something hits you on top of the head, not all that hard but it startles you.

"Hey!" comes a voice from above.

You look up to see the face of a man staring down from over the top edge of the roof behind you. "Climb up," he says. "And make it quick!"

It's then you realize that it was the end of a rope that struck you. It dangles down the wall, thick and knotted every couple of feet to ease the climbing. A *deus ex machina* if ever there was one. Not that you're complaining.

If you let Grant climb first, turn to page 132.

If you take the rope and climb, turn to page 138.

Northbound it is.

The undead population here is much thinner than in the area you have just left behind. A few zombies shuffle about aimlessly until you get within a dozen yards or so of them at which time the moaning sounds they make intensify and they head in your direction. They are slow and easily avoided, though. There is no point in shooting them. It would only be a waste of ammo. And you definitely do not want to be low on ammo if you ever come across the insane thing—or one of its ilk—you encountered at the entrance to the apartment building. The very thought of it leaves you a bit shaken.

Halfway to the next intersection you pass a church to your right, an elegant, stone building with a jutting steeple on top. On Sundays you can hear the bell within the steeple ringing out from your apartment. A surprising touch of melancholy mingles with the strange amalgam of emotions swirling about inside of you as you realize that it's very possible you may never hear the church's bell ring again. You stop and approach the house of worship as you notice someone has spray-painted a biohazard symbol on the building's stone face next to the front doors which are made of wood. And below the symbol is a message: *Beware the Howlers*.

You think about the mad creature you've only recently left behind, the torment burning in its eyes. The way it screamed at you and Grant. The way it *howled*...

"No truer words," you mutter.

"What's that?" Grant gives you a look.

"Nothing," you say. And then you move on.

The air is warm and still here. You are sweating from your previous exertions. It feels as though the alcohol is already beginning to wear off. It seems that a healthy dose of fear and adrenaline will sober you up in a hurry. You think about where you are and where you're going, what little information you have at your disposal as far as the big picture is concerned: What are the authorities doing? Right now, as you walk along this nearly desolate street? What will you find if and when you make it out of the city? The northern border is generally regarded as the great river that runs from the west to the east there. It's only a few miles away but under present traveling conditions it could take a long while to get there. And what will you find if—no, *when*—you get there? The army? More zombies? Nothing at all? Too many questions. And really no answers at all. Hopefully you'll run into someone else who has more information about what the hell's going on than you do. In the meantime you have to keep moving. And hope for the best.

You approach the next intersection, take in the sounds of general mayhem erupting from the city in all directions: screaming, alarms, a distant, muffled explosion. And then, from the right, the high-pitched sawing sound of a dirt bike's engine. The guy riding it races into the intersection about five paces in front of where you and Grant are standing. He isn't wearing a helmet, is dressed only in a pair of shorts, tennis shoes, and a T-shirt. He's going pretty fast, at least thirty or forty miles an hour. You can tell there's obviously something wrong with him by the way he's leaning to one side on the seat, like he might just fall over at any—

And there he goes. The bike does a flip and slides twenty feet or so before coming to a stop. The guy rolls across the pavement a few times, flopping about like a rag doll until he runs out of momentum and lies face down in the street.

"Oh, damn," says Grant as he starts to walk over to the guy. When you get there, the guy isn't moving. His head is turned at a weird angle. Eyes open, glazed, staring at a whole lot of nothing. The skin has been torn free in patches from his legs and arms, the result of his less-than-polite introduction to the pavement. *Oh, damn* is right.

"Now where do you think he was going in such a hurry?" asks Grant.

You give the only answer you can think of: "Same place we're going. The hell out of town."

The bike's engine, miraculously, is still running.

Grant lifts the bike, stands it up on its wheels once again, gives the engine a rev. "Could use a new paint job," he says once the noise subsides, "and the handlebars need a little straightenin' out." He circles around and straddles the front tire, holding it tight between his legs. Then he pushes and beats on and generally pummels the handlebars for a minute or so, eventually releases the tire from his leg lock, gives a nod of satisfaction and says, "There, that oughta do."

"Oughta do for what?" you ask.

"For ridin'," he says, smiling at the look on your face. "You know, to get us outta here."

"You know how to operate that thing?"

In response, he swings a leg over the seat, sits down, revs the engine again. "I most certainly do. Thought for a time about going pro, back in my younger days. Then one day I broke both my collarbones and decided it might not be the best career choice after all."

"How reassuring."

"Come on then," he says, patting the seat behind him, looking over at you and offering a grin that could only described as maniacal. "I promise I'll take it nice'n'easy."

If you figure it can't be any more dangerous than making your way through the city on foot, turn to page 134.

If you tell him there's not a chance in hell you're getting on that thing, turn to page 168.

"I think barricading ourselves in is a terrible idea," you say. "Grant's right. We'll be trapped. And sooner or later, those damn things are gonna find a way in. We need to go. Now. While we have a chance."

"Hell, yes," says Grant. He's all one big grin. "Front door then?"

You shrug. "Why not? At least we know what's out there."

You pull the second box of cartridges from your back pocket, start to reload the .38.

"Well, you two have fun," says Jack. He leans his shotgun against a stack of boxes, grabs a keg, drags it over and pushes it up against the back doorway. "As soon as you're through that door I'm doing the same there. And I'm not opening it again. You sure you want to do this?" He's looking straight at you.

No, you're not sure at all. You're not sure about much of anything, truth be told. But your adrenaline's up. And you've already said your peace, so...

"Yeah, I'm sure."

"Okay, then" says the proprietor with a genuine look of concern on his face. "It's been nice knowing you. And I really do hope you make it. I got one shell left on me. All I had underneath the bar. When you open the door, stand aside. I'll see what kind of path I can clear."

Grant pats you on the shoulder. "Ready to do this?"

You give him your most intense and level stare. "Ready as I'll ever be." And you try to convince yourself that it's true.

"Okay, then. On the count of three." Grant reaches for the door handle.

"One... Two... *Three!*"

He pulls the door open and moves to the side.

And there they are, three zombies that made their way in and around the bar, that are waiting there to greet you. Jack's shotgun roars. Two zombies fall back. Well, the one that took the brunt of the blast actually *flies* back a ways. The third zombie takes a bullet in the head from Grant's handgun, slumps to the floor.

"Go! Go! Go!" shouts Grant. You go through. Grant follows. You hear the door slam shut behind you.

Other than the three zombies that were at the door, there are only four more that have managed to enter the establishment up to this point and these have not yet reached the bar itself. You approach the counter, over by the taps, take aim at the nearest of the zombies with your .38, and fire. Its head snaps back and the creature collapses to the floor. Grant comes up beside you and fires off a few shots of his own. Within moments, the three walking dead men and the one woman are walking no more.

"Like fish in a barrel," says Grant. He gives you a light push. "Let's go."

The two of you circle out and into the main room of the building, make your way past the tables with their chairs resting upside down on top of them.

"Wish we had time for a game of pool," says Grant. "Woulda been fun kickin' your ass."

You appreciate him trying to add some levity to the situation. It helps with the fear a little. But your heart is still beating heavily and rapidly in your chest.

The collective moan from the undead gathered outside flows into the pub through the shattered window. Arms reach in with grasping hands, some of them missing a finger or two. But, thankfully, you don't hear the tortured howling sound that you've quickly learned to dread. If it's only the slow moving moaners outside, then the two of you might just stand a chance of getting away. A pretty good chance, you tell yourself. And try to force yourself to believe it.

"All right, I'll go through first this time," says Grant after the two of you reload your weapons. He gives you a toothy grin. "Only fair, now isn't it?" His accent is thicker than usual. Could it be his own fear driving it to the surface?

"On three again. You pull the door open. I'll go through. And you follow. Sound like a plan?"

Not much of one, you tell yourself. But aloud you say, "Sure, sounds like a hell of a plan."

Grant's grin widens. "You're a terrible liar. Anybody ever tell you that?" He turns away before you can answer. "So here we go then... One... Two..."

You undo the deadbolt.

"*Three!*"

And then you pull open the door.

Grant lets loose with an animalistic growl and practically leaps through the doorway, firing his gun. A second later, you go through too, pulling the door closed behind you. Guess it will be up to Jack if he wants to come out and reset the deadbolt.

There are zombies approaching from every direction. The moaning, battered, walking dead, most of which display injuries no living person could hope to survive, let alone continue to stay on their feet after sustaining them. Yes, there are a lot of zombies. But not as many as you feared their might be. You have room to maneuver, to bring your gun up and aim, to fire and move on to the next target. To keep moving, keep moving, to try and cut a northerly path through the shambling creatures around you.

"Conserve your ammo," shouts Grant from just ahead of you and to the right. "Try to dodge 'em, if possible. Shoot only when absolutely necessary. We keep firin' like this and we'll run outta bullets before we reach the intersection."

It's sound advice. You find it relatively easy to avoid the grasping fingers of many of the undead. On more than one occasion, a zombie manages to brush its fingers across the exposed flesh of your arms. One of them actually gets a light grip on your shirt sleeve before you bring the gun up and shoot it in the face, so close that it's impossible to miss. The gas mask dangles from where you wrapped it around your left arm. You count shots, reaching into your pocket for more cartridges as you come close to having to reload once again.

"Looks like it clears out a little ways ahead," says Grant in a near shout from beside you. "Stay the course and we'll be free of this before–"

A torturous howl cuts him short. From directly ahead of you. In the very direction you and Grant have been heading.

"Oh, Christ," he says.

You couldn't agree more.

"Fall back!" Grant says. "Fall back!"

"Fall back to where?" you wonder aloud.

The remainder of the crowd before you parts and there it is, the howler, coming straight toward you in a near run. A wide gash across its forehead has painted its face in a mask of blood. One of its arms hangs at a weird and very painful looking angle. It is a woman. Hair cut short to the bottoms of the ears. On the left side of her neck you can see a very vivid tattoo of a black star. Somewhere along the way she lost her shirt, is dressed only in a white bra and a pair of black pants. Her right foot is bare, the left adorned in a white tennis shoe.

"I don't know," say Grant in answer to your query. "Just... back!"

The woman howls again. She comes at you in an odd, jerking gait. You fire at her head. And miss.

"Gut shot!" says Grant. "She's still alive. Take her down!"

You shoot her in the torso. So does Grant. The woman keeps howling. Slows. Only a little though. The both of you fire again. And then she is there, maybe five feet in front of you. Your .38 comes up, points toward her face. You pull the trigger. *Click!*

"Oh, no."

The woman comes closer. Turns toward Grant. Leans forward. He fires twice in rapid succession into the woman's stomach. She stops howling. The terrible sound cuts off like a siren suddenly deactivated. She closes her mouth then opens it wide, like she's about to howl again. But, instead, she exhales...

A misty, dark cloud issues from her mouth. The cloud rushes forward, spreads out, and disperses. But not before enveloping Grant's head for a second.

Grant lets out a choked, coughing sound like someone is strangling him. Without thinking, you swing your gun hand around and into the side of the howler's head, hit her solidly with the butt of the gun directly above the ear. She staggers but doesn't go down. And so you hit her again. And again. Finally, she collapses.

You turn to Grant, see that he is standing there, his hands to his throat, face turning a startling shade of blue. It's obvious he's having trouble breathing. You want to help him but you don't know what to do. And, besides, there are still plenty of zombies around and they are closing in once again.

"Come on," you say and grab Grant by the elbow. You half guide, half pull him forward as quickly as you can, lash out with the gun at any hands that reach out for you.

And then you are free. You have reached the intersection. The crowd of zombies is behind you. Luckily, there are no cars coming through the crossroads or the two of you may have been run over. From the east you hear the awful cry of a howler. Not too close but not nearly far enough away, either. You have no urge to head in that direction. To the north you can see another pack of zombies gathered beneath the next flashing yellow traffic light. To the left, or west, the way looks relatively clear.

Grant coughs and gasps for breath as you try to decide what to do.

"Keep moving," Grant manages to say in a gasping wheeze. "Got to keep moving. Find help."

As you watch, an ambulance pulls to a stop a few intersections down to the left, lights flashing on its roof, its siren emitting a solitary *whoop*. Good to see that not all of the emergency workers have fled the scene. And just like that, your decision is made.

Turn to page 156.

You grab the rope, push it toward Grant. "Go. Now. I'll try to stall them." You can't believe you just said that. When did you become so heroic? Not that you've ever really had many opportunities to prove your bravery before now. Truth is, like most people, you've never found yourself in all that many life-threatening situations. And now that you're presented with one... Well, it seems that you're quite the courageous individual after all. Who knew? Although the sight of all those zombies and the two howlers at the front of the pack make you want to find some place cozy and safe and never come out again. But seeing how that isn't even remotely an option, you figure you'd better get down to the business of buying you and Grant some time. And there seems to be only one way to accomplish that.

The two howlers approach the Dumpster, are now only a few feet away. The one on the left, the male with the open wounds crisscrossing his flesh, reaches for the Dumpster's lid, obviously getting ready to pull himself up.

"Uh-uh, close enough," you say, hoping you manage to sound like some semblance of a badass, even if you are the only one who hears it. With that you raise your trusty ol' .38 snub nose handgun, aim for the zombie's head just as he starts to climb up to where you stand, and pull the trigger. Your aim is true. The bullet punches the zombie in the face, snapping his head back. He falls to the ground, out of sight, still screaming from where he lies on the pavement. You swing the pistol over to where the female howler is approaching the Dumpster but she ducks down, hidden below the edge of the yellow garbage receptacle upon which you stand. You step forward, toward the edge of the lid, closer to the undead horde that clogs the alleyway all the way back out to the street. Looking down, you aim the gun in the direction you expect to find the female zombie. But she isn't there. Movement from your right distracts you and you turn just in time to see the female popping up around that side of the Dumpster, her arm swinging toward you in a throwing motion.

The chunk of asphalt strikes you on the side of the head, just above the temple. It isn't a particularly large projectile but carries enough speed and mass to hurt you and knock you off balance, to cause you to stumble forward just... far... enough...

And then you're falling, face first toward the concrete below. The gun flies from your grip as you extend your arms and try to use your hands to break your fall. You break something, all right. Your left wrist. It snaps with an audible cracking sound and then the rest of your body slams down onto the ground. The wind is knocked from your body and you're pretty sure your nose is broken and maybe a few teeth have been knocked loose from your face smacking into the ground's unyielding surface. There is pain everywhere. So much of it calling for your attention. Too much to think about, really. But it's nothing compared to what comes next. Because the zombies, they are on you, and they are hungry. Somebody yells your name and it takes a moment to think of who it might be. Oh, yeah. Grant. Probably safe up on the roof by now. Your body is used in a seeming tug-o-war of the undead. Hard to tell who is winning this grisly little game. It seems as though there are about to be a number of victors, actually. The joints of your hips and shoulders pop. Knees. Elbows. Amid all the moaning you can hear the sounds of your clothes being ripped to shreds. Something screams, wildly, insanely. Is it you or one of the howlers? You're not really sure. The undead creatures pull at you and bite at you, so many hungry mouths. This is pain beyond imagining. It would be nice if your brain would do you a favor and let you go into shock. And look at that. It does. Everything goes numb. Dreamy. It isn't long before the world fades to black.

Well, red first.

And then black.

THE END

You hop on the back of the motorcycle before you can decide to do the sensible thing and change your mind.

"Now hold on tight," says Grant back over his shoulder. "Wouldn't want you to get shaken loose or anything like that."

Before you can tell him that that's not going to happen because he's going to drive nice and slow, he revs the engine one more time and pops the clutch. You get your arms around Grant's waist just in time to keep from falling off as the front wheel comes up off the ground and the bike takes off like a rocket.

"What the hell are you doing?!" you shout, the rushing wind tearing the words out of your mouth.

"Relax! I've got it all under control!" Grant shouts back. Then: "You mind loosenin' up a bit. I can hardly breathe!"

You don't loosen up. In fact, your grip gets a little tighter as you see the flashing light of an approaching intersection and realize that Grant has no intentions of slowing down. At least, not by much. Just enough to lean the bike to the right and turn toward the east, engine screaming all the way.

"Where are you going?!" you wonder aloud in spite of your fear and rising anger.

"Zombies ahead! Figured I'd try an alternate route."

You zip along the right hand side of the road. A couple of cars pass by going in the opposite direction. Looking to either side of the street, you see a handful of pedestrians, some of them carrying arm-loads of what you can only assume are prized possessions, making their way along the sidewalks. It seems that you and Grant are far from the last two people to decide to vacate the city after all.

Another blinking yellow light ahead. Grant slows down a bit–not nearly enough for your liking–before pulling out into the cross-roads and swinging the bike to the left–northbound again–with a sudden opening of the throttle. You approach another intersection, slow down, continue north with another burst of speed. Traffic is still light in this area although the number of pedestrians seems to be increasing. At the next intersection, the light is not blinking. It is green. Grant blows through it without slowing down at all. You can hear him laughing. Like the grin he showed you earlier, the sound is quite maniacal.

"At this rate," he shouts, "we'll be outta the city in no time at all!"

Yeah, if the lunatic doesn't get you killed first.

Past the next intersection the road is crowded with shambling figures. There is an overturned car in the middle of the street. You can hear the sound of inhuman howling over the bike's engine.

"More zombies ahead!" Grant informs you, in case you didn't notice.

He turns left at the green light, hardly slowing at all as there is no oncoming traffic. The sound of the bike's engine echoes off the fronts of the buildings that line either side of the next section of roadway. The next light is red. The bike slows, but does not stop. There's nothing coming from the south so Grant rolls out into the intersection, turns right, and lets the bike tear up the blacktop.

"Another green light!" says Grant, indicating the intersection looming a hundred or so yards before you. "The gods must be smilin' upon us."

Beyond the intersection the way looks clear. Maybe the gods *are* smiling. Grant races up to the intersection. As you enter the crossroads, you detect movement to your right. Something big. Fast. Everything happens so quickly.

The car running the red light clips the rear wheel of the motorcycle. You leave the seat, your grip around Grant's waist broken. The time you spend in the air lasts maybe a second. And then you're hitting the pavement. Hard. Bouncing. Rolling. Sliding. Rolling again.

Stopping.

The pain is beyond anything you've ever experienced in your life. There's just too damn much of it. It feels as though every nerve ending in your body is singing in agony. Thankfully, you black out. Not for long though. How long? Who can tell? But the pain's still there when you come to, just as bad as before. You black out again. Come to. All the while, your vision's blurred. Clearing a little bit with each revival. Things are swimming into focus now.

You're lying in the road. On your side. Your arm is angled strangely beneath you. So is one of your legs. You blink and the world comes a bit more into focus. Grant is lying about ten feet away. Blood is leaking out his ear, painting a trail down across the side of his face. His eyes are open, staring at you. Not seeing you though. Not seeing anything at all.

"Grant," you say, or try to. "You son of a bitch." It comes out as more of a gargle. Your mouth is filled with blood.

A pair of feet step into your field of vision. Dirty sneakers. One of them untied. Then another pair. A woman's high heels. One of the heels is broken off as are a few of the toenails. The ones that remain are painted pink. Then there are more legs. More shoes. The sounds of moaning. Other than your own, that is. You feel yourself being lifted. Maybe a foot off the ground. Then dropped. You scream and black out again.

When you come around this time, you feel something biting into the muscle of your left forearm. Something else is gnawing on a calf muscle. Then there is more biting. The tearing away of your flesh. Moaning.

You black out one more time.

Fortunately, you don't come around again.

THE END

Consumed with fear, you turn and grab the rope, start pulling yourself up, sure that at any second the howlers are going to come rushing up onto the lid of the Dumpster and drag you back down.

"Hurry, damn you! Hurry!" yells Grant from just below you. And you do hurry, climbing with a strength and speed you never knew you had. Nearly overwhelming terror really is one hell of a motivator, now isn't it? The knots in the rope aid in your ascent and you're nearly halfway up when you hear Grant shout, "Off to hell with you then, you bastards!" There is the sound of gunfire–two shots... three–and then there is nothing but screaming and moaning and the screeching of the howlers.

In a matter of moments, you reach the top of the wall and with the muscles in your arms burning, and the help of your rescuer, you pull yourself up and onto the roof. There you turn and look back down over the edge, hoping against hope to see Grant following your lead.

No such luck.

Yeah, that screaming you heard, it was his. And you know that if you were in his place you'd be screaming too. The zombies have him. Somehow, they've gotten him off the Dumpster and onto the ground. They are pulling at him, pulling him *apart*, leaning in to bite and tear at his flesh with their mouths.

"Grant! Oh, God!" you shout just as he goes under beneath the sea of the undead, washed away like a drowning man caught in a riptide, his body never to be found again. It is a horrific sight but you can't look away, feel as if it's your duty in some way to bear witness to this terrible scene. If you had not been so quick to grab the rope... If you had let him go first...

Then it would be you down there, now wouldn't it? Sure, you cannot help but feel some measure of guilt over what has happened, but at least you're still alive to feel it. For now, that is. For now.

As you watch, one of the howlers, the male with the ragged wounds across its torso, pulls itself free of the crowd and rather nimbly climbs up onto the top of the Dumpster. It looks up at you, leans its head back and emits that awful screaming sound. Then it grabs the rope and starts to pull itself upward.

The man on the roof with you, also leaning out and staring at the action below, curses then turns and walks back to where he has anchored to rope around the base of a large TV satellite dish. He tugs and pulls at the rope, cursing some more as he finds undoing the knot he has created a bit of a struggle. You look back down and see that the zombie is making steady progress toward the roof.

"Don't worry," you say. "I got it."

Then you pull free the handgun which you tucked back into the top of your jeans to make your escape from the undead mob below. The howler looks up at you and screeches, emits what looks like a cloud of black gas from its mouth, just as you take aim into the center of its face and pull the trigger. The gun kicks in your hand and the mad creature plummets to the dumpster below, slamming down flat on its back. It doesn't move. The members of the undead mob take little notice of the proceedings, preoccupied as they are.

You walk over to your rescuer just as he undoes the knot. He makes quick work of reeling in the rope. He's a big guy with a beard and a head full of unkempt hair dressed in jeans, brown boots, and a red flannel shirt with the sleeves rolled up.

"Sorry about your friend," he says when the rope lies in a short, thick loop at his feet.

"Yeah, me too."

"No one should have to go out like that."

"You're unarmed?" you ask.

He gives you a look. "Yep. Ran out of ammo a while back. Ditched the gun. Wasn't going to do me much good like that. Why you ask?"

"Just wondering... why you didn't do anything."

His look darkens. "I saved your ass, didn't I?"

"Yeah, I guess you did."

"Trust me, if there was anything I could do, I would have done it. Just like you, right?"

You lower your eyes, say, "Well, thanks for helping out." Then you head off across the rooftop, away from the alley and the Dumpster. And Grant. Or what's left of him. Probably very little by now.

"Where you going?" asks the man with the rope.

"I don't know," you tell him without looking back. "Out of this damn city."

He laughs. "Good luck with that. Me? I'm staying up here. Safest place you can be, you can count on that. Wait until they come in and clean the place up. Wait for someone to come rescue me."

You keep walking. "Good luck to you too."

Is it just your imagination or does the afternoon air seem slightly cooler up here? A number of buildings are butted one up against the other in this part of town, the rooftops stretching away before you for a few blocks at least. Just to the right and ahead of you is a small metal structure with a door set into it, housing what is most likely the top of a staircase that leads down into the building below.

If you want to continue along the rooftops, turn to page 152.

If you decide that you want to try the door, see if you can make your way back down to the streets, turn to page 162.

You decide to wait, see how this whole thing plays out. Trying to break out is a ridiculous plan. They have guns. You don't. And that's all there is to it.

The time passes slowly within the tiny room. The two of you don't talk much. There really isn't all that much to say. You wonder what's going on out there, beyond the walls of the church. Intermittent sounds make their way into the room through the tiny window. An occasional explosion. Sirens. Muffled shouts and screaming. Slowly, imperceptibly, the light coming in through the window fades away. The minutes tick by. Hours crawl past. The window goes dark.

And, eventually, they come for you.

There is the sound of the door being unlocked.

"If you see an opportunity, a chance to get away, take it," Dora tells you under her breath.

The door opens. There are three of them. Armed, of course. Dora is led out of the room first, then you. Down the hallway, back out into the main area of the church, past the first line of pews, over to where the old priest had addressed you earlier from behind the pulpit. Randomly placed candles have been lit, filling the area with an ethereal, flickering light. Just behind and to the right of the pulpit sits a rectangular, wooden altar with three brass crosses set into the front of it. Draped across the top is a white cloth. You are led up and told to halt before the altar. Coming around the other side is the old priest. His daughter stands behind him. The rest of the priest's followers form a loose wall behind you and Dora. You glance back over your shoulder; there are a lot of guns pointed your way. This is definitely not good.

The priest is handed something from his daughter that gleams in the light of nearby candelabras. It is a long, ornate, ceremonial dagger, its blade tapered with an edge that looks wickedly sharp.

My god, they're going to sacrifice us. The idea sends a chill down your spine. A sick feeling takes hold of your stomach. You look around, a bit more wildly this time, readying yourself to make a break for it. The priest raises the dagger high over his head. He is talking about God's will, about being chosen to end this undead plague that has gripped the city, which threatens to consume the world, about how he is more than ready to perform the task that is required of him.

Panic threatens to overwhelm you. This can't be happening. It all seems too surreal. As if a zombie plague overrunning your home city wasn't enough to swallow for one day, now you're about to be sacrificed to God by a crazy man who believes he is the world's chosen savior. It's all too much. You have to do something. Now.

Apparently Dora has reached the same conclusion. Without warning, she turns and launches a nose shattering punch into the armed man standing directly behind her, then she is a blur of fists and feet, elbows and knees, performing one of the most impressive displays of fighting skill you've ever seen—and you've watched your share of martial arts films. Six people go down in no time at all. Judging by the way they stand around and watch, most of those assembled there are just as impressed by what they are seeing as you are. But, soon, they move into action. And there are just too many of them. Dora is taken down by what has to be at least ten people in a fairly well coordinated assault. You receive a blow to the back of your head, a pistol whipping that dazes you, hurts you, disorients you, and succeeds in preventing you from getting any crazy ideas of your own.

"Bring her to me!" shouts the priest in a surprisingly loud and strong tone of voice.

Dora is carried, struggling, over to the altar, laid atop it on her back, arms and legs pinned down by four men, a fifth standing next to where her head lays, pointing a pistol into the center of her face. He jams the barrel of the gun down into her forehead. "Stop moving. Now!" he hisses at her.

Dora struggles for another moment then, obviously realizing the futility of the action, lies still.

The priest smiles down at her. You watch all of this in mounting horror, trying to clear your head of the cobwebs that seem to be clinging to your brain since that little love tap you received.

"Don't you understand?" the old man says. "This is an honor of the highest order for which you've been selected. With your help, we will save the world."

Dora is unimpressed. "Eat shit, you crazy old freak!"

The smile fades from the priest's face. "Ah, well. If this is the way it must be, then this is the way it—"

There is a loud thumping sound like God himself has decided to knock on the outside wall of the church. The ground shakes. Bright light streams in through the stained glass windows set into the wall behind the altar.

"What was—" someone starts to say.

Then there is heat and more light, as hot and as bright as the sun. Someone else, it seems, has decided to handle the zombie plague in their own way. In less than a second the roof of the church is lifted up and away. The walls explode inward. A monstrous roaring sound fills the area where you stand, consuming the whole of your world, the universe. The very particles of your being are cast asunder in a blast of explosive fury.

And that, as they say, is that.

THE END (In a big way.)

After barricading the doors with full kegs of beer, the three of you head up the stairs with Jack leading the way. At the top, there is another door which Jack opens and steps through. Beyond, there is a short hallway which turns to the right, leading onto another, longer stretch of hallway. A couple of closed doors and open archways line the hallway here. After locking the main doorway, Jack walks past both you and Grant then through the first open archway to the left. The room beyond is the main living area. Two windows with white blinds and dark curtains pulled halfway open face out onto the street that runs north and south in front of the building, the very roadway you and Grant used to get to Jack's Place. The same roadway from which the zombies are at this very moment invading the bar where you were only just recently enjoying a rather tasty beer. In the corner of the room ahead of you and to the left is a large TV, its face angled out so that it can be easily viewed from any spot in the room. Tall, thin, very modern looking speakers stand to either side of it. There is a couch and a couple of chairs, one of them a comfortable looking recliner. The floor is wood and there is a large brown and white throw rug laid out in front of the couch. A dormant lamp hangs from the ceiling over the center of the room. To your left you see a bookshelf loaded with books, the spines of which you cannot read in the dim lighting from where you stand. Next to the TV is a sleek, black, glass fronted cabinet filled with audio/video components. There are a couple of potted plants on small tables near the windows. Portraits of cityscapes done in black and white adorn the walls. To the right is another open archway beyond which you can see part of the kitchen.

"Nice place," Grant says as the three of you wander into the room.

"Thank you," says Jack as he heads over to one of the windows where he uses a thin, long, white plastic rod attached to the blinds to open them. "Nothing too extravagant, but I like to live comfortably."

As he speaks you and Grant walk over and stand to either side of him. The view outside and below is pretty much what you are expecting to see. The street is fairly crowded with the wandering dead. Most of them seem to mill about aimlessly, even bumping into one another on occasion before turning and setting off in other directions. On the sidewalk in front of the building, however, things seem to be a bit more organized. Zombies are gathering in front of the place where the shattered window would be in what can only be described as an orderly fashion. At the edge of the street near the sidewalk, you can see the howler which took the direct blast from the shotgun lying there, unmoving, next to a parked car. Zombies pass by the dead howler, giving it little to no attention at all. As you watch, one of the walking dead actually trips over the dead howler's outstretched arm, just barely managing to stay upright.

"Let's check the back," says Jack. He turns away from the window and heads back across the living room, through the archway and out into the hall. He opens the door set into the wall there, motions for the two of you to follow. Inside is what looks like a small den. There are more bookshelves here and a desk with a computer monitor perched on top of it near the left wall, a high-backed, leather office chair behind the desk. Directly across from the doorway is another window, this one covered by closed blinds also. Again, Jack opens the blinds and the three of you peer through them.

You are presented with a view of an alleyway. At the present time, it is mostly deserted. Looking along its length, you can see where the alleyway dead ends only a short distance away before a looming brick wall. There is a dumpster down there near where the back door of Jack's Place would be. The angle does not allow you to see where the mouth of the alleyway would be to the north, your left. There are only two zombies wandering around down there. As you watch, though, a third figure walks into view. As if sensing that it is being watched, it stops and looks up toward the window. Even from here, you can see that there is something different about this newcomer, something in the way it moves and cocks its head inquisitively.

"I think we've got ourselves–" you start to say. Just as the newcomer opens its mouth wide and emits that terrible screeching sound you've heard far too much of recently. The closed window mutes the sound a bit but even still it seems unnaturally loud, too loud to originate in the small frame of the woman creating it. As the sound eventually dies down, you finish by saying: "Another howler."

"Looks that way," says Jack and he walks back out of the room. "Help me reinforce the front door."

He leads you to another closed doorway, opens it and steps inside. "Come on then," he says and you go in. "We'll use this."

You're in a bedroom. It is a relatively Spartan area with a queen sized bed, a dresser, and not much else. He pats his meaty hand down on top of the dresser which is a big, intimidating, oaken beast of a piece of furniture. "This should keep them at bay for a while should they get through the doorway below."

It takes a couple of minutes for the three of you to maneuver the dresser out of the room, down the hall, around the corner of the L-shaped corridor, and over to the main entranceway. Once it is pressed firmly against the doorway there, Jack smiles and says, "All righty then. Anybody else hungry?"

Forty-five minutes later finds the three of you sitting around the rectangular, metal topped table in the kitchen, enjoying one of the finest meals you can remember eating in a long time. The light in the ceiling is on, powered by the generator on the roof. Half-full glasses of red wine stand next to each of your plates. Grant is saying how he really isn't much of a wine drinker but this is some damn fine stuff. "And the food... I think you missed your calling, Jack. Should have opened a restaurant instead."

While the meal was being prepared, you and Grant took turns looking out one window and then another. Slowly the back alley grew more crowded with zombies during that time. The situation out front remained pretty much the same. The undead milled around, most of them seemingly unwilling to participate in any sort of invasion of the pub. Apparently, with no prey in sight, there was nothing prompting them to attack. As time passed, you became increasingly relaxed, more and more convinced that Jack's plan was a good one.

"We'll just wait it out here," he said while he cooked. "By tomorrow, the authorities should have things under control, I would think."

"And if they don't?" you had wondered aloud

"Well, that's a bridge to be crossed when we get to it," said the big man followed by: "Food's ready. Let's eat."

The food, the wine, the conversation... All of it has combined to further relax you. This was definitely a good idea. Safer by far—and much more comfortable—than being outside, roaming the streets among the undead.

You finish your meal, lean back comfortably in your chair.

That's when you hear a loud crashing sound from somewhere below.

And just like that, the good mood that has managed to fill the room disperses.

You and Grant jump up from your seats. Jack stands a bit more slowly. "Now, let's just all take it easy. Even if they did manage to get through one of the lower doors, they'll never be able to—"

A screaming, howling sound comes echoing down the hallway. You pull your gun out and follow Grant down the hallway. You stop where the dresser is pushed up against the doorway, listening to the howling sound coming through the door. Something bangs against the door. Hard. Again. Again. You aim your gun over the top of the dresser. Jack comes up behind you and grabs your arm, forces it down.

"Don't do anything stupid," he says. "They're never gonna get in here."

The banging and the howling stops. After a few moments of silence, Jack says, "See. That thing has figured it out too. Nothing to worry about."

There is a moaning sound. Low at first, then increasingly louder. Not just the moaning of a lone zombie but two, three, then too many to discern. The howling starts up again, farther way, from down near the bottom of the stairs you imagine.

"What are they doin'?" asks Grant. The door starts to creak. Your heart skips a beat as you're sure it's the sound of the hinges opening. But the door is still closed. Of course it is. The zombies don't have a key, and you doubt they have any real lock picking skills either. You relax, just a bit. There is that creaking sound again. And then you get it.

"They're going to push the door in," you say. "Take it right off the hinges. Right off the frame."

Jack is shaking his head. "None of them are strong enough to do that."

"Not individually, no. But get enough of them... ten... twenty... all pushing in unison. All pressing toward the doorway... All that combined weight... It's not like they have to breathe or anything. And that door, it's gonna give, eventually."

"No way," says Grant.

The creaking is replaced by a loud cracking sound. And the door does indeed come free of the frame, pushes the dresser back a couple of inches. That moaning sound is louder now, coming in through the opening around the doorway. The howling is louder too.

You reach over the dresser and fire at the door. Grant does the same. The two of you squeeze off round after round until you're pulling the trigger on an empty chamber.

"Oh, Jesus," says Jack and he turns and flees back into the apartment, goes into the bedroom and locks the door behind him.

You approach the door through which the big guy has disappeared, pound on it. "What are you doing? Open up!"

"Go away!" he shouts. "Find your own place to hide."

You and Grant exchange a look.

"A place to hide?" says Grant incredulously.

You run into the living room, look out the window, toying with the idea of going out one of the windows there. But the street down there, it's teeming with zombies now. Apparently, the word has gotten out–in whatever way the undead creatures might possibly communicate–that there's fresh meat inside Jack's Place. And it looks like the zombies are ready to party.

You go into the den and check the window there, hoping against hope... Same situation. The alley is crowded with dead folks and it looks like most of them are heading toward the doorway that will take them into the storage room. And up to the apartment above.

There is a loud crunching, banging sound as the dresser goes over and the door of the apartment's main entranceway falls inward.

And then Grant and you are in the hallway, loading your guns, firing at the first zombies that come around the corner. Firing at the next wave. And the next wave after that. Reloading and firing, firing, firing...

Until the rounds run out.

After that, you discover that there really is no place to hide.

They grab Grant in the hallway. Catch up to you in the kitchen. And as those moaning faces, those reaching, grasping hands close in, you hear another door crash inward followed by the sound of Jack screaming from his hiding place. You smile, just a little, taking some perverse pleasure in the man's pain. That's what he gets for leaving you and Grant to fend for yourselves. The feeling doesn't last long, however. The agony of what comes next doesn't last all that long either. Although it does seem to go on and on and on...

It's all just a matter of perspective, really.

THE END

You are in no hurry whatsoever to head back down to street level. The guy who rescued you was right when he said that up here was definitely a much safer place to be. It's tempting to just stay up here and hope for rescue too. But you can't bring yourself to do it. You need to get out of the city. As quickly as you can. Who knows how soon the authorities will regain control of the situation? If ever. Wait around for that and you might be waiting an awfully long time. Might as well find out how far the rooftops can take you.

As you walk you are able to see tendrils and columns of smoke drifting upward into the sky at various distances across the city. There is the sound of an explosion off to your left somewhere, not close enough to cause you any great worry. The rapid popping of gunfire can be heard too. Sirens wail in various directions and someone's car alarm is bleating on a nearby street. Just the general sounds of the mayhem that has descended upon the city where you live.

The soundtrack for the apocalypse, you muse. *Welcome to the end of the world...*

As you walk you pass two more of the small, square structures with the doors set into them, keep walking past the final one all the way to the northernmost edge of the last building along your rooftop journey. You figure you'll take a look down and see the state of things below. If it looks fairly sedate, you suppose you'll head back to the doorway you just passed and make your way down. If not? Maybe you'll wait things out for a little bit, hope that any chaos in the area will either disperse or move along.

The roof here has a low, three foot high wall running along its edge. You approach it, gun once more tucked into the front of your pants, barrel pointing downward. Then you place your hands on top of the cement wall, lean out a bit and assess the situation below.

The street down there is nearly vacant. A lone SUV goes driving by. There is a man standing on the sidewalk across the road from you, head tilted back, hands cupped around his mouth. "Karen! Karen!" he shouts at the building before him, one in a long row of what appear to be office buildings for the most part. In two different places, a large biohazard symbol has been painted on the fronts of buildings in florescent green.

As things seem to be relatively under control here, you figure it's a good time to make your exit. You can't stay up here forever, after all. It's probably best that you take advantage of whatever positive situation arises. You are thinking about turning around, heading back to the metal structure with the door set into it, seeing if there's a way to gain entrance, head down past the floors below you to the street outside, continue your journey out of this godforsaken city...

That's when you hear the raised voices. From your left, a group of what must be about twenty people comes running into the street. "Hurry!" someone cries out. "They're still behind us!" You see that "they" most certainly are. A smaller group of figures pursues the fleeing group of humans. By the strange, limping ways in which they run it is obvious that these are howlers giving chase. One of them is bent completely over, using both feet and hands to carry itself along in an odd, apelike manner. Now you can hear that horrible screaming sound you've become all too familiar with, a lone cry that is immediately echoed by several others in a terrible chorus of the damned. The humans pass by directly beneath your vantage point then continue on toward the intersection a block away to your right. The screamers go the same way. It isn't long before a crowd of the slower, shambling dead enter the scene from the west, their random moaning sounds occasionally layering one on top of the other, amplifying the idiot, awful sound within the walled confines of the roadway. There must be upward of forty of the hobbled creatures. The sound and the sight of them might be piteous if it was not, in fact, so disturbing.

Mesmerized as you are by the great mass of the undead nearing the point of the street over which you stand, you do not even notice the helicopter until it is a mere twenty feet above your position, hovering through the force of its whirring blades above the crowded street below. It is a sleek, black machine with short, stubby wings on its sides, their only purpose—as far as you can tell—to serve as mounts for the long, extremely wicked and efficient looking weapons mounted to their undersides. The aircraft drifts out until it is directly over the middle of the street then its nose dips noticeably downward. And that's when it unleashes hell on the utterly defenseless, walking dead. The machine guns mounted beneath each wing open fire with a stunning ferocity. Zombies fall to the ground as they are shredded by the gunfire. Limbs are torn from bodies. Heads explode. As you watch, a tall zombie in a runner's outfit is cut completely in two at the midsection. It is an awesome sight only topped by the launching of a missile into a group of half a dozen of the undead. The explosion sends chunks of bodies of all sizes and descriptions raining down in a circle thirty feet across. Definite overkill there. Seems like whoever's in the helicopter is just getting their kicks. So caught up are you in watching the carnage below that you fail to notice the helicopter drifting farther toward the other side of the street, that its nose has slowly but surely swung around in your direction. Another missile is launched, this one impacting near the base of the building atop which you stand. The roof shakes beneath your feet and your hands slip from where they have been pressed down on top of the wall. And just like that, you go over. It's a thirty foot drop to the sidewalk below. Survivable, possibly, if you land feet first and happen to absorb the impact just right. No doubt there would still be a number of broken bones. Probably a number of other rather serious internal injuries. All pointless conjecture, however, due to the fact that you're taking a headlong plunge. The ground comes up fast and then it's lights out. Probably for the best, really, as surviving a fall like that would have undoubtedly left you terribly injured. And that would have only lead to a lot more suffering before the end finally came.

THE END

You lead Grant the couple of blocks over toward where the ambulance awaits. As you near, the driver's side door opens and a woman of medium height and build, somewhere in her early thirties with red hair tied back behind her head, wearing the white shirt and dark pants of an EMT, exits the vehicle, looks off to the south and raises something to her face with her right hand. Grant wheezes and continuously tries to clear his throat. It is a painful sound and you would not be surprised if he started spitting up blood at any moment. You think about what the howler did to him, of what it might mean. Of what it more than likely *does* mean. Hopefully the EMT will be able to do something about it.

"Excuse me," you say rather loudly as you reach a point about twenty feet away from the female ambulance driver. From here you can see that she holds a tiny digital video recorder to her eye. She jerks the recorder from her eye and snaps her head around in your direction, obviously a bit startled.

"My friend needs help."

You can also see from here that the woman has a belt with a holster buckled around her waist. She switches the camcorder to her left hand, pops free the thin leather strap that holds the gun at her side secure within the holster.

"God damn if everybody in this city doesn't have a gun," you say.

"Everyone that's left, for sure," says the woman as she pulls the weapon free. "Wouldn't have made it this long without one, I don't think." Her gun is now leveled at you and Grant. "You might want to think about stopping right where you are. Another step and I'll *make* you stop."

You have your empty .38 in your hand, think about threatening the EMT with it before discarding the idea. You need this woman's help, after all. Getting into a "who's got the bigger gun?" standoff probably isn't the best way to go about acquiring that aid.

You raise your right hand, point the gun toward the sky. Pulling on Grant's arm, you bring him to a halt about ten feet from the woman.

"I'm not here to cause any trouble," you tell the woman. "I need your help. My *friend* needs your help."

"Yeah, I can see that," says the EMT. She does not lower the gun as she brings the DVR back up to her eye, aims it at where you and Grant stand for a few seconds, lowers it again. "But, unfortunately, there's nothing I can do for him."

Grant starts to cough violently then falls to his knees. Surprised, you lose your grip on his arm. He kneels like that for a few moments then topples over onto his side, hacking so hard that you're sure he's going to tear something inside.

"What do you mean, you can't do anything for him?!" you ask the woman, startled by this sudden worsening of Grant's condition. "You can't just leave him like this."

"Oh, I can," says the woman. "And I will. As a matter of fact, I'm not getting any closer to him than this. And if you were smart, you'd stay away from him too. No, actually, you'd put a bullet in his head and end his suffering."

You look at her in shocked amazement. "Are you really a medical professional?"

"Yes, I really am. Or was. Not sure if I'll still have a job after all this. If I live through all this, that is."

"Look... Please..." You're not sure what you should say at this point. "Those... *things*... Those howlers... One of them did this to him."

Grant is still coughing, squirming about on the ground. Surely he can't keep coughing like that for much longer.

"Yeah, I'm perfectly aware of what has happened to him. It was either a howler or the two of you just came out of the stain. But you're moving in the wrong direction for that. Although, I see that you do have a gas mask."

"A guy was selling them..." You shake your head. "Look, we have to do something. We can't just stand here and—"

"No, *you* look!" The woman's voice is suddenly harsh. "There is nothing that can be done. Not that I'm aware of. Maybe they've figured something out by now. Out there, somewhere outside the city. But that's not going to do us any good in here. My partner... Albert... He got a face full of that... whatever it is those things carry around inside of them. The same stuff that came leaking out of that lab, it seems. The same stuff that turned this city into a great big zombie breeding ground. And it did the same thing to him. I tried to save him. Did everything I could think of. Which wasn't all that much, to be honest with you. The change... It happens so fast. In another few minutes, your friend there, he's going to get back up on his feet. And he's going to start howling. That phase... I think it lasts for an hour or so. And during that time he's going to try to infect others. He's going to try to infect *you* if you let him. Exhale that stuff into your face, the same way it was done to him. Then that phase of the disease will pass. And he will fall down again. He will die. The next time he gets up and walks around he'll be one of them. One of the living dead. A zombie."

You're shaking your head from side to side, but just what it is you're trying to deny you don't know. Because all the while the EMT's been speaking you've been stepping away from where Grant is lying, a little bit at a time, without even realizing it. The thought of breathing that stuff, of becoming one of *them*... It's just about the most awful thing you can imagine.

"So that's it then," you say. "I've got to let him die."

"No, there is one other alternative. Put a bullet in his head, show him some mercy. It's what I should have done for Albert, poor bastard."

The woman lowers her gun, turns and walks toward the ambulance.

"Where are you going?" you ask. "You can't just leave. Aren't you supposed to help people? Isn't it your job?"

She laughs.

"Like I said before... Not really sure if it's my job anymore. But, hey, if you need a ride, well, come on then. Guess I can't just leave you stranded out here. Now that would be downright cruel."

"But what about–"

She waves a hand dismissively. "Leave him." She takes another step toward the ambulance. Stops. Turns to look your way again. "Actually, no. Hold on a minute."

Grant is still lying on his side, coughing. He rolls onto his back, stares straight up into the sky. He takes in a deep, sucking breath, holds it. Releases the breath with a squealing sound like that emitted from the pinched opening of a balloon. He repeats the process. The coughing fit starts to subside.

"Ummm. There seems to be something happening here," you say loudly enough for the EMT to hear. You look back toward the ambulance at the sound of one of its rear doors swinging open. The EMT disappears inside for a moment, reappears with a wooden stretcher under her arm. She jogs the short distance from the ambulance to where Grant is lying. Her gun is in its holster; the DVR is hanging from a plastic cord around her neck. Now she has a gas mask of her own in one hand. She sets the stretcher on the ground next to Grant, tells you that it would probably be a good time to put your mask on as she pulls hers down over her face, adjusts the straps that hold the thing onto her head. You do as she suggests, fumbling with it a bit, trying to make it fit as comfortably as possible, which really isn't all that comfortable. "Hopefully the filters are good on that thing," she says, her voice muffled by the mask, and nods in your direction. Then she shrugs. "If not, you'll find out the hard way."

How reassuring.

"Help me out here."

You stick the gun back into your pants then walk over and stand beside her. "Grab his feet. I'll get the shoulders. We need to lift him onto the stretcher."

Wondering at the woman's change of heart, you do as you're told. Maybe circumstances haven't robbed her of all compassion.

It takes only a few moments to complete this task. Then the woman uses the black straps that are attached to a series of holes cut into both sides of the stretcher to tie Grant down–one strap across his ankles, another across his waist which also secures his wrists, another across his shoulders, and the last one across his forehead.

"All right, now let's get him into the back of the ambulance."

The two of you lift the stretcher and its securely bound occupant, carry it over to the ambulance as quickly as possible. Once Grant's inside, the woman closes the back doors of the vehicle, checks to make sure they're secure. Then she circles around toward the driver's side door, tosses a "Get in" back over her shoulder.

You head toward the passenger side, open the door and climb up onto the empty seat.

Moments later, the woman is guiding the ambulance through the intersection, heading south.

"Where are we going?" you ask. "We need to get out of the city. The river is less than a ten minute drive to the north of us. We can cross one of the bridges there. Find help. Be done with all this craziness."

The woman is shaking her head in denial. "There's something I gotta do first. Something I gotta see. If I'm right, it's something that the whole world will want to see."

The road ahead is free of traffic and the ambulance picks up speed.

If you want to get out of the city *right now*, turn to page 174.

If you decide to go along for the ride and check out what the EMT thinks is so important, turn to page 192.

You decide to try and head down into the apartment building below. Walking over to the last of the small metal structures on top of the roofs over which you've traipsed, you are pleased to discover that the door has a fist sized rock placed between its lower edge and the frame, preventing it from closing, more than likely put there by the man with the rope who rescued you. Probably should have shown a little more gratitude toward the fellow but some of his comments really didn't sit well with you. Ah, well, you're sure he'll get over it. More to worry about lately than some hurt feelings.

Opening the door, you find that it does, indeed, grant you access to the top of a staircase that will take you down and into the building below. The stairwell is nearly identical to the one you used to exit your own apartment building, doubling back on itself between floors. You prop the door open as far as you can to allow as much light as possible into the stairwell as the electricity is not working here either. Then you start to make your way down. You pass the third floor, then the second, seeing no point in stopping at either level. The darkness down here is nearly complete and so you walk slowly, carefully, dreading the possibility of losing your footing and twisting an ankle. Or worse. It won't be much fun trying to make it out of the city with a serious injury of any kind. Things are going bad enough as it is.

Upon finally reaching the first floor landing, you grope around and locate the handle that will open the door and grant you access to what you assume is the lobby beyond. After pulling free the gun tucked down the front of your pants, you open the door and step through, pistol held out before you. And discover, immediately, that you are not alone.

The lobby is small and dimly lit, much smaller than the one in the building where you live. Set into the wall to your left is a single elevator door. Directly across from you is a beige, featureless wall. And to your right is the building entrance, a single metal door which is open, allowing the light from outside to drift into the room, the lobby's sole source of illumination. Gathered near the door are five people, all looking out through the doorway. Nervous as you are due to your recent confrontations with the undead, your finger tightens on the trigger. Before you can fire, though–if that really is your intention—one of the members of the group glances your way, turns to face you, and says, “Hey, guys, we’ve got company.”

The others turn and it becomes readily apparent that none of them are zombies—it’s in the way they move and the fact that they all appear to be healthy and whole. One of them is a woman, young, with long, blonde hair pulled back behind her ears and spilling down over her shoulders. She wears a white tank top, dark sweat pants and black running shoes. In her hands she holds what appears to be a heavily modified, sawed off, double-barreled shotgun with a large ammo clip jutting out of the bottom of it. Every member of the group is armed and you suddenly find five different firearms of various makes and models aimed your way.

“Lower the gun,” says the woman in a calm and level voice that seems quite used to issuing orders. “Now.”

Not seeing that you have a lot of choice in the matter, you do as you’re told.

“Drop it.”

You do.

“And kick it over here.”

You comply once again. A man standing next to her crouches down and takes the gun.

“Good. Now march your ass on over here so we can get a better look at you.”

With a sigh, you walk away from the doorway, one careful step at a time. Halfway across the lobby, the woman tells you to stop where you are. “You fellas thinking what I’m thinking?”

A guy to her right, the one who spotted you first, lets loose with a laugh and says, “Oh, hell yes.”

It’s the woman’s turn to laugh. “I figured as much.” She takes a couple of steps toward you, both barrels of her weapon aimed at your stomach. A pull of one of those triggers, at this range, and you’d have a hole in you big enough to throw a football through.

“You see, Jerry here—” The woman jerks her head in the direction of the man who’d so adamantly agreed with her. “—just lost himself a little bet. Very unlucky for him. But then you show up and, just like that, his luck changes back the other way. Funny how things work out sometimes, isn’t it?”

You don't say anything, just stare back at her.

"Not much of a talker, are you?" She smiles, an expression you can just make out in the room's rather anemic lighting. "No biggee. All that really matters is whether or not you're a good moaner."

The others laugh. You don't like the sound of any of this.

"Eric," she calls back over her shoulder.

"Yeah, boss," says a tall guy standing just inside the entranceway.

"Take one of them down."

"Not a problem."

As you watch, the man steps into the rectangle of light coming in through the entranceway, raises a rifle with a scope attached, places the butt of the gun against his right shoulder, aims out through the doorway, lowers his eye to the scope, then fires. The rifle jumps with a *crack!* and one of the other men standing next to him let out a "Woo-hoo!" someone else says. "Sonofabitch doesn't *miss*."

The woman never takes her eyes off of you through all of this, never lets the gun in her hands waiver. "How's it look out there?" she asks.

"Few stragglers. That's about it." This from the man with the rifle. "Nothing else too close to the body."

"Jerry. Nick. Bring it in. Eric. Marty. Keep 'em covered."

"Aw, damn," says Jerry. But that's the extent of the protest as he and the man who had let loose with the celebratory shout dash out through the entranceway.

Your mind is racing, trying to figure out just what the hell is going on here and what you might be able to do about it. Not much, it seems, as long as those shotgun barrels are aimed your way.

Everyone is quiet for the next minute or so and then Jerry and Nick come hustling back in through the entranceway, a dead zombie carried between them; one of the men is holding the arms, the other the legs They drop the body on the floor just behind where the woman is standing. The corpse appears to be that of a middle aged man dressed in what is left of a very ragged looking three piece suit.

"You know what to do," says the woman. Jerry and Nick set about stripping the body down to the waist. Once this is finished, the man previously identified as Marty says, "All right, now step aside." The other two men need no further prompting. They stand back as Marty pulls a hunting knife with a very sharp looking six inch blade from a sheath hanging on his hip, kneels down and starts to cut away long strips of flesh from the naked torso of the dead body. You look away, not wanting to witness the grisly procedure. The woman chuckles. "Oh, trust me," she says. "You ain't seen nothing yet."

Within minutes, Marty has laid a thick pile of flesh across the legs of the dead zombie. He stands and walks over toward where a duffel bag sits near the elevator door. Unzipping the bag, he removes a towel from inside and goes about the task of cleaning his knife and hands as best he can.

"All done?" asks the woman.

"Yeah, I think we've got enough there."

"OK, then." She steps to the side and motions toward the body with her shotgun. "Move," she tells you.

Not sure what it is that's going on here, but liking it less and less with each passing moment, you walk over and stand next to the body. It is an awful sight, even in the dim lighting. The corpse's eyes are open, staring up at you from beneath the hole in the center of its forehead where Eric's bullet found the mark. There is what looks to you like an accusatory expression on the thing's face. Not that you could blame it after the recent indignities it has suffered. Most of the skin of its torso has been cut away, revealing red muscle underneath. The skin lies in ragged strips across the corpse just beneath the belt it wears. You take in deep breaths, willing yourself not to be sick, but almost immediately regret it as the smell of the desecrated thing at your feet washes over you.

The woman walks up behind you and pushes the twin barrels of the gun she carries into the small of your back. "Put it on," she tells you.

The words make no sense to you whatsoever.

"Excuse me?" you say.

"The skin," she says with exaggerated slowness. "Pick it up. Dress yourself in it. Make yourself as much like one of them as you can. Because—and trust me on this one—your life depends on it."

The dread and disgust you feel morphs into something deeper as the woman's words begin to sink in. These people want you to use the dead flesh carved from the body lying at your feet to disguise yourself as a zombie. Obviously they are mad.

"Why are you doing this?" you ask, not surprised by how thin your voice sounds.

"I would think that it's obvious by now," she says. "You're our little guinea pig. If the disguise works, then we'll all be doing it. It was going to be Jerry but now you get to be the first one to try it out. Think of it as a new fashion statement. One that's sure to be a big success. At least, you better hope it is." She chuckles. "Kind of gives new meaning to the question: 'So who are you wearing?'"

The others laugh, Jerry a bit louder than the rest.

"You're all crazy," you tell them

"Maybe, yeah," says the woman. "But we're also the ones with the guns. Now quit wasting time and put the damn skin on."

If you refuse to do as you're told, turn to page 172.

If you do as instructed, realizing you have no choice in the matter, turn to page 178.

"Suit yourself," says Grant with a shrug. He revs the engine again. "I'm going to go check things out. If the way ahead is clear. I'll come back and let you know."

With that, he pops the clutch and takes off like a shot.

"Good riddance," you say, more than a little angry at this desertion. "I hope he wipes out and breaks his neck." You don't really mean it though.

And so you walk. Alone. Listening to the sounds of general mayhem emanating from all points of the city it seems. You head north, the same direction Grant just took. He's already lost to view, the buzzing sound of the motorbike swallowed by the surrounding din. Gunshots are being fired somewhere in the near distance. A siren wails. A car zips through the intersection directly ahead. You keep your gun in your hand, dangling at your side. It'll be a damned miracle, you figure, if you make it out of the city without having to use it.

Just beyond the next intersection, you can see a thick crowd of figures milling about. This cannot be good news. You quicken your pace, plan on taking a left and heading westbound at the crossroads, make your way north again when a clear route presents itself. As you reach the crossroads, a big, primer-grey pickup truck comes roaring up, abruptly stops in the middle of the intersection. There are three men in the bed of the truck, all of them shouting and whooping and hollering. One of them tosses a beer can onto the street. The three men stand up, aim firearms of various descriptions toward the thick crowd of figures in the near distance, and on some unspoken command open fire. You're all of about fifteen feet from the truck. The cacophony is rather impressive. Figures can be seen falling to the street where they are struck by bullets. The men continue to laugh and holler, obviously enjoying themselves a bit too much given the circumstances.

You start to jog to the west, wanting to get away from this scene as quickly as possible. That's when a police car comes squealing around a curve in the near distance, races up and stops less than a block away. You stop too, stuck halfway in between the pickup truck and the police cruiser. An amplified voice issues from the black and white car ahead: "*You there, in the truck, cease firing immediately!*"

Quite miraculously, the gunfire does stop. You take this as a good sign. Until the three men turn and aim their weapons out over the roof of the truck toward the cruiser. Someone yells, "Screw you, pigs!" And with a roar of the engine and the squeal of tires, the truck takes off. Directly toward the police car.

Another amplified warning: "*Stop the vehicle. Now!*"

As you watch you see the doors to either side of the police car spring open. Two officers climb out, use the doors as shields. They have pistols in their hands. And they don't waste any time using them. *Pop-pop-pop!* go the gunshots. The men standing in the back of the truck return fire. Everything is happening so quickly. The truck has covered maybe half the ground between you and where it was previously parked. It rapidly gains speed, closing the distance. You're standing off to the side of the road, at the edge of the side-walk. Out of the path of the truck, but with all these bullets flying around...

As you watch the truck's windshield cracks on the driver's side. The vehicle immediately veers wildly out of control. Heads directly toward the place where you've been standing, undecided, trying to figure out what you should do, where you might be able to hide. You turn and start to run but it's hopeless, really. The truck runs you down before you can take three steps. The initial impact is crushing, feels as though the great, snarling, metal beast has shattered about every bone in your body. Then the wheels are going over you and it's all over pretty quickly at that point.

THE END

You chastise yourself for being silly. It's just the fear, the adrenaline, the general confusion of the situation... You have no way of knowing if one way will be any safer than the other.

You follow Dora.

Of course, you two aren't the only ones who've decided to escape this way. There are a couple of people running ahead of you. A few more enter the tunnel behind you. Good thing one of those in the lead has a flashlight or else the place would be pitch dark. You'd lose your bearings instantly, more than likely spend your time crashing into one wall and then another. Even with the light guiding your way, it isn't long before you're completely disoriented. It's nearly impossible to keep track of the direction in which you're headed down here, especially during a mad flight like this.

You stomp through ankle high water at one point. Cross a rattling, grated metal bridge. Pass through a corridor that is practically raining with foul smelling moisture. Run along a thin walkway set just above a rushing stream of sewage. And all the while there is the screaming, the wailing of the howlers as they give pursuit. The acoustics down here are warped, unpredictable. Sometimes the screaming seems to come from directly ahead of you. At these times you almost stop, *want* to stop more than anything in the world. But everyone else keeps running so you continue onward, ever onward into the seemingly endless labyrinth of the sewers.

And then the person with the flashlight *does* stop.

"What's... going on..." you gasp as you pull up behind Dora. And then you see. A ladder. Just like the one you used to enter the sewers. Already, the two figures you've been pursuing for what seems like a very long time, but in actuality can only have been a few minutes at most, are clambering and clanging up the rungs. Dora looks at you, gives you a slight shove, pulls her gun free of its holster.

"Go," she says. There is a look in her eyes... You know it would be pointless to argue. Grabbing the lowest rung, you start to climb.

A third of the way up you hear other footsteps coming down the tunnel, convinced that the howlers have arrived. But, no, not yet. More escapees. Looking down, you see that Dora is sending them up. You call her name.

"Keep going," she replies, her voice filled with the reverb of the tunnels. "I'll be up shortly."

A few more rungs. The screaming, loud now. Only a short length of tunnel away. Louder still, seemingly from directly below. Dora's gun erupts. One, two, three times in quick succession. Silence falls as the echoes fade away.

"Dora?" you call out even as you continue to climb.

A pause, then: "Yeah. I'm fine. Keep going."

A sound from above, grating metal as the manhole cover is pushed away. Light streaming down into the hole, warmer, more natural than the light you've been following. You look up, trying to look past the man climbing above you to see what's going on with the man above him, the one who lifted the cover. But what gets your attention is not what you see up there, it's what you hear...

Moaning.

An unholy chorus of it.

Only a large gathering of the undead could make such a sound.

Then there is screaming. From above. Terrible, agony filled screaming. And something drops, bangs off the rungs near the top of the hole. A grunt and the man above you is falling, slams into you with plenty of force to knock you free of the ladder. And then you are falling onto the person below you, and the next one down, twenty-plus feet to the floor of the tunnel next to where Dora is standing.

The impact breaks something in your leg, your right arm. The weight and the force of the two bodies slamming down on top of you cracks something in your chest, your skull.

There is a sound. An explosive sound. So loud. The loudest thing in the world. Another explosion. Random thoughts flitting through your mind... Dora... The gun... Howlers...

But there is just so much pain. You black out. And never come back out of it.

THE END

No. This is too much. Sure, you want to live, you want to survive all of this... this *lunacy...* that's overtaken the city that's been your home in recent years. That has, in the course of a single day, been transformed into an unrecognizable and nightmarish place. A place where the dead walk and feast upon the living, where gun toting maniacs attempt to force you to wear the skin of the undead. You should have stayed on the roof. Hell, you should have stayed in your apartment. Things may have not turned out any better in either of those places but at least you would have been spared this indignity.

"I won't do it," you say.

The gun presses with more force into your back.

"Last chance," says the woman, her voice still calm and even. "Put the damn skin on."

Sweat runs down from beneath your hairline as you see the men before you step toward either the entrance or the elevator door.

You clear your throat. Swallow. Take a deep breath. "I told you I won't do it."

"Well, then," says the woman's voice from behind you. The pressure of the gun in your back lessens just a bit.

She won't shoot me, you tell yourself. *Sure, she might be crazy. But she's not* that *crazy.*

"Looks like it's not your lucky day after all, Jerry," she says.

"Well that really sucks," says Jerry.

And that's when the woman pulls the trigger.

The blast *does* rip a hole right through you. The exit wound... Oh, yeah, it's a big one all right. You collapse to the ground next to the defiled body already laid out on the floor. The pain is just too big and too overwhelming to comprehend. A black fog swirls through your mind. The pathways of your nervous system short circuit one after the next. The all-consuming agony drifts away as you are consumed with shock. Mercifully, it all ends rather quickly.

THE END

"Screw that," you say and pull the .38 out of the front of your pants, aim it at the woman driving. "Turn this thing around right now. Head north. I've had enough of this place. I've had enough of zombies. And howlers. And all the rest. I want out. You're going to take me to the river or I swear to God I'll spray your brains all over the window next to you and drive out of here myself."

With the mask covering her face accept for the two clear circles over her eyes, it's impossible to read her expression, to have any idea how she is reacting to this threat. You hope you came off effectively enough. It's not every day that you tell a woman that you're going to bring a violent end to her life. And it's not something that you're at all sure you could go through with. Even if the gun was actually loaded.

The woman looks your way for a moment, sees the gun pointed, unwavering, at the center of her mask. With a slight nod of understanding, she slows the vehicle at the next intersection, waits for a couple of cars to pass by, then turns the ambulance around and starts to head back the other way.

Okay, you tell yourself. *Things are looking up now.* Well, not for Grant, unfortunately. But you're well on your way to getting out of the city, to surviving this awful day. You lean back in the seat, lower the gun so it's aimed at the driver's midsection.

"Just keep driving," you tell her, "and I promise I won't hurt you."

The vehicle passes through the intersection where the two of you loaded Grant into the back of the ambulance. It's not much longer before Grant starts howling.

The sound is loud, ear-piercing within the confines of the vehicle. And it's not the only noise issuing from the back of the ambulance. Without thinking, you turn and look to where Grant is lying strapped to the stretcher on the floor. Various medical tools and machines are secured to the walls, most of which you have no earthly idea as to their use or function. Grant is flopping about, trying to break free of his bonds, actually rocking the wooden plank up in the air from side to side, from top to bottom, causing it to bang and clatter relentlessly on the floor beneath him. As you turn back, ready to ask the EMT if there's anything she can give Grant to calm him, she chops down on your wrist with her right hand, a powerful blow that sends the gun flying from your hand and clattering onto the floor down by the woman's feet. Then she grabs you behind the neck, slams on the brakes, and pushes you forward with everything she's got. The ambulance wasn't traveling all that quickly but the push combined with the sudden lack of motion from the vehicle throws you forward, hard, into the dashboard. You catch the brunt of the impact with your shoulder and the right side of your jaw. Stunned, you crumple backward, half on the seat and half on the floor below. You really should have put your seatbelt on. Those things do save lives, you know. The EMT is obviously aware of the fact as she has hers secured around her.

Still dazed and groaning from the force absorbed by your jaw and your body, you feel the hard end of the EMT's gun press into the side of your head. "Take the mask off," she says, her voice muffled but clear enough to understand. "Now."

You reach up with your left hand and do as you're told.

With her free hand, the woman pushes the button that lowers the power window next to you. "Toss it outside."

You do.

"Get in the back."

She motions with the gun. You do not like where this is going. Not at all. But what choice do you really have? There's plenty of space in between the two front seats to make your way into the back of the vehicle. The EMT disengages her seatbelt and follows close behind you, the gun pressed into your back.

Your shoulder is throbbing and your head is only just beginning to clear. Grant is still throwing his fit, struggling to free himself from his bonds but failing so far. The EMT stays near the seats, prompts you to get down on the floor next to where Grant is thrashing about. When you look back at the woman you see that with the hand not holding the gun she is lifting the camcorder to her eye.

"Lean over him. Yeah, just like that," she says as there is a lull in Grant's howling.

A red light comes on near the camera's lens.

"Now wait. Shouldn't be long now."

And it isn't. Grant howls once more. Then he coughs. And exhales...

A dark mist rushes out of his mouth and envelopes your head, positioned only a foot or so above the face of the prostrate man on the floor. Surprised by the dark breath that has escaped him, you involuntarily breathe in. This is a mistake. Suddenly your throat is burning and it feels like something has reached down inside of you and is squeezing your lungs.

And so it begins. The terrible transformation. You can't get enough air. Gasping and wheezing, you reach for your throat. All the strength seems to flow out of your body and you collapse across Grant's still struggling form. A distant voice is talking, telling someone, somewhere, to watch, just watch. This is how it spreads. This is what they have wrought. Someone must be held accountable. Something must be done to make amends. But what could possibly amend something as terrible as this...

The words fade beneath the pain that consumes you. Time melts and transforms, loses all meaning. There is nothing but pain. And a lack of air. Never enough air.

The voice returns. *Do you see? Do you see?* And then: *I'm sorry for this.* And: *You have suffered enough.* There is an explosion of sound. The struggling form beneath you goes still. You find that you've reached a point of the transformation where you can breathe a little easier now. You open your mouth, wide, suck in a great draft of soothing, cooling air. And you *howl...* Oh, you howl.

There is another explosion of sound.

A nanosecond of agony beyond comprehension.

And then nothing at all.

THE END

"Fine, I'll do it," you say and you kneel down next to the corpse. Reaching out, you take one of the strips of flesh between your fingers, start to lift it but then shake your hand and let it fall.

There is laughter from the others.

"Looks like we got us a squeamish one," says one of the men.

You reach for the strip of flesh again with similar results. The act of peeling it away from the other strips fills you with revulsion. You just can't do it.

"Marty," says the woman from behind you.

After placing his knife in the sheath hanging from his hip, Marty approaches the body from the other side, leans over and grabs the whole pile of flesh in his hands

"Stand up," he tells you. He steps over the body and comes up next to you. "Hold out your arms." You do as you're told and he begins to wrap the dead skin around your arms which are bare below the sleeves of the T-shirt you wear. He applies it randomly, letting some of the strips hang loosely. A feeling of revulsion courses through you but you manage to not pull away and allow the "disguise" to continue to be applied. Once your arms are sufficiently covered by the foul stuff, strips of the flesh are pressed to and wrapped about your neck and then stuck in patches to the skin of your face. Marty then takes the remaining flesh in his hands and wipes it on various places on your clothing. After this, he uses his knife to cut and tear your clothing, adding to the authenticity of your disguise. Eventually, he steps away, looks you over and gives a thumbs up to the woman still standing behind you.

"Turn around," you hear her say. "Let me get a look at you."

You turn in a full circle. She smiles. "Not bad. If I saw you looking like that out on the streets, I wouldn't hesitate to put a bullet in your head. Now, the question remains: can you act?"

The feeling of the zombie flesh adhering to your body distracts you and at first you're not sure what she's asking of you.

"Go on," she says with a jerk of the gun in her hands. "Act like one of those monsters. Convince me you're one of the undead."

"What?" you manage through your confusion and disgust.

"Why?"

"Well, if you can convince me then I think you'll be able to convince those stupid creatures. At least the slow ones. The howlers? That might be another story. We'll just have to wait and see."

So you do as you're told. You let your arms hang limply at your sides, let your head tilt at an odd angle, start to moan and walk slowly toward the woman, one leg dragging slightly behind you.

She gives you an appraising nod. "You know, that's not so bad. Although I wouldn't come any closer if I was you. That whole zombie getup's making my trigger finger a little jumpy."

You stop where you are and drop the zombie act.

"How's it look out there?" asks the woman.

"Still a little thin," says one of the men–you think it's Eric.

And so everyone stands around and waits. Five minutes go by. Ten.

"Looks like things are starting to heat up." It's the same guy talking.

You can hear the sound of a large vehicle rumbling by. Then there comes the sound of screaming. "Oh, yeah, here they come."

The woman approaches you, gestures toward the door with the gun. "Okay, then. Looks like you're on."

She has you turn around and walk toward the doorway. Your heart starts to beat heavily in your chest.

"Here's what's going to happen," the woman is saying. "You're going to take fifteen steps out that door. Exactly fifteen. Take one more and we'll cut you down. Then you're gonna stop. And you're gonna do your best to convince those things that you're one of them. Got it?"

The thought of going out there... All feelings of disgust are forgotten. You breathe deeply, trying to fight the fear climbing up your throat.

"At the appropriate time I will shout further instructions to you," the woman says and then asks once again: "Got it?" She prods you in the back with her gun.

"Yeah," you manage to say. "I got it."

You're standing in the doorway now. Before you is a cement walkway running outward through ten feet or so of lawn at the far edge of which it intersects with the sidewalk. Beyond that is the road which is quickly filling with the walking dead.

"All right. Time to do this." The gun pushes you hard in the back. With that you step through the doorway, force yourself to put one foot in front of the other even though every instinct in your body is telling you to turn around, to run back into the apartment building. But, of course, that is simply not an option. Remembering what you're trying to do here, you start to drag one leg behind you. And you begin making the ubiquitous moaning sounds of the walking dead. *Four steps,* you tell yourself. *Five. Six.* You're breathing heavy now. You can feel the sweat running down your back. The urge to run is practically irresistible. *Eight steps. Nine.* The street is thick with zombies. It looks like a damn zombie exodus of some kind. Where are they going? Are they in pursuit of something? Or running away from something? Do they even know? *Eleven steps. Twelve.* A couple of zombies pass within three feet of you. Two more walk by. *Fourteen steps. And... fifteen.*

You stop. And you stand there. And you wait. For what, exactly, and for how long you don't know. But you're pretty sure you'll find out soon enough.

Turn to page 188.

What have I got to lose? you tell yourself. And so you duck under the railing and head off in the same direction Tony just went. You have a gun. You'll follow at a safe distance and at the first sign of potential trouble you'll turn and hightail it out of there as fast as you can.

The air is cool there in the shade of the trees. A breeze blowing in from the direction of the river rustles the leaves. The sounds of traffic are muted here, nearly fading completely the further you go. It's easy to imagine that you've already left the city, maybe stepped through some magical gateway like in C. S. Lewis's famous tale and ended up in some other world filled with strange beasts, gallant knights and beautiful princesses. The fantasy does not last for long, though, as the wooded area is small and you soon find yourself emerging out the other side. The last of the trees stands a mere twenty feet or so from the river's edge. There you see four people standing, waiting—quite impatiently, by the looks of them—near the boat Tony told you about. It's a rowboat. A green, metal rowboat. It sits in the water a few feet out, bobbing slightly in the tiny waves lapping at the bank. A black chain leads from the boat's prow to a thick, iron spike that has been driven into the ground a few feet from the water. The spike has a metal hoop at the top which the chain has been fed through and secured to with a padlock. This prevents the boat from drifting away. And from being stolen by anyone tired of waiting for Tony to return and row them out of there.

He stops and turns back around to face you. "*Voila!* Am I not good to my word?"

You can only stare in disbelief. "Oh, you've got to be kidding me."

Tony folds his arms across his chest, flexing his muscles and giving you a stern look. "It may not look like much, but I assure you, it will get you to safety."

You look at the other people gathered there. A middle-aged man and woman stand near one another. The man has his hands on the shoulders of a young boy in front of him. To the left of this small family is a blonde woman in her twenties and to the right is a dark-haired man of about the same age.

"Can we go now?" asks the blonde woman, hands on her hips in a pose of impatience.

"Yeah, I think that would be a wonderful idea," says the man standing behind the young boy. "No telling when one of those damned dead things will sniff us out. Or one of those howlers will show up."

The people gathered here are obviously afraid. Well, all of them except Tony who seems to be holding up just fine. The ones who are waiting for him to take him out of this place, though, wear the sweat and the grime of their ordeals on their skin and clothes. They've obviously been through quite a bit. And they are ready to put this nightmare behind them.

"Well?" says Tony, looking only at you.

"Let's do it," you say. Reaching into your pocket, you pull out your wallet, hand over the cash. After the transaction is completed, Tony pulls a key ring from a pocket of his shorts, squats down next to the metal spike and unlocks the chain. Then he pulls the boat halfway onto the shore.

"All right," he says. "Everybody in."

The boat has three benches: a long one at the stern, one of equal length across the middle, between the oarlocks, and a small one, just wide enough for one person, at the prow. The family sits one next to the other along the stern bench. The young woman sits down on the bottom of the boat between them and the middle bench. The young man makes himself as comfortable as possible between the middle bench and the prow leaving you the small, one person bench next to him. Behind you, Tony uses his considerable strength to push the heavily weighted boat out onto the water. Then he takes a few splashing steps through the water before pulling himself up and over the side of the boat, next to one of the oarlocks, dangerously rocking the vessel and nearly causing it to capsize. But, somehow, it does not go over, and before long Tony brings the boat under control with the oars, gets it turned around, and starts paddling for the far bank.

You are sitting at the front of the boat with your back toward your destination, and so you look past the people seated in the boat and watch the near bank slowly drift away. Tony puts all those muscles in his back and arms to good use, propelling the boat across the river at an admirable clip. Looking to your right, you can now make out the bridge to the east that you were hoping to find. It doesn't look too far away and you figure you would have reached it in ten minutes or so. But it appears as though a number of large vehicles are parked on the bridge. Military vehicles by the looks of them. And you have to wonder just how easy it would have been getting out of the city there. The situation seems to be the same along the bridge you see to the west a bit farther away. You tell yourself that you made the right decision after all.

From behind you comes the buzzing of a small motorboat. Turning your head you see it zip away to the west. A few moments later, the rowboat is rocked by the wake generated by the speeding boat. There are general gasps and concerned comments at this but Tony reassures everyone by saying, "Not to worry. Not to worry. It will take a lot more than that to send this little baby over."

Downriver, beyond the westerly bridge, you can make out the stern of a massive, square-faced ship approaching. You watch it long enough to reassure yourself that it is moving much too slowly to intersect the rowboat's trajectory. At least, you hope this is the case. Because a boat of that size has way more than it takes to flip Tony's "little baby" hull side up.

You turn your attention back to the receding bank, surprised by how far away it is now. The rowboat has to be near the center of the river already. You wonder how deep it is here. Thirty, forty feet? Deeper? You really have no idea. It's not something you like thinking about too much. All that dark water down there. And what might be lurking within its depths.

Some sort of monster? you ask yourself, trying to make light of the idea. *Ready to reach up and pull the rowboat down into the wet and the blackness where it lives?* Now you're just being silly.

There is a *thump* that rings out through the hull of the boat. A number of people cry out and you feel your breath catch in your chest. The monster...

Another *thump.*

Tony stops rowing.

"What the hell was that?" asks the older man sitting at the stern of the boat.

"I'm sure it's nothing," says Tony, always the optimist. "A bit of drifting debris. A piece of wood maybe." He reaches back with the oars, ready to resume rowing.

And that's when the rotting hand reaches up out of the water and grabs onto the edge of the boat, between you and the starboard oarlock. The boat rocks. People cry out. There is another decayed hand, reaching up next to the first one. Tony pulls the gun out of his pocket, yells, "Sonofabitch!" then proceeds to beat at the hand nearest him with the butt of the gun. Following his lead, you pull out your .38 and do the same to the hand nearer to where you are sitting. The hands eventually let go, disappear back into the water. Everyone sits and waits for a minute, peering into the river.

"Okay, everyone just relax," says Tony. "I think it's gone."

He reaches for the oars again.

Yet another thumping sound and then there are more hands. A pair of them. Two pair. A third. All reaching up out of the water and pulling on the same side of the boat. As overburdened as the small vessel is to begin with it goes over. And then you are in the water. Trying to swim in all your clothes with your shoes on. Feeling the tug of the current. You come up from underwater, breach the surface, look around for some sign of the boat, for your fellow passengers. The boat is already downriver about twenty feet, floating upside down. You see a couple of people splashing around next to it, reaching toward it. You think you can see Tony trying to pull himself up and onto its rounded hull. Kicking off your shoes, you start to swim in the direction of the boat. Something grabs your leg. And down into the river you go.

You struggle against the grip on your leg, manage to slip free for a moment. Then something else grabs hold of your other leg. Then there are hands on your arm. On your shoulders. Further and further down into the murky depths of the river you go. The distance you can see in any direction is only a couple of feet at the most. A leering face comes out of the surrounding darkness, flaps of skin dangling where its cheeks should be. Your lungs are starting to ache from the constant struggle and lack of air. But that pain is negligible compared to what comes next as hungry mouths start to bite into you at various places along your body.

Drowning *and* eaten alive by the hungry dead. What a truly terrible way to go. Talk about your bad luck.

THE END

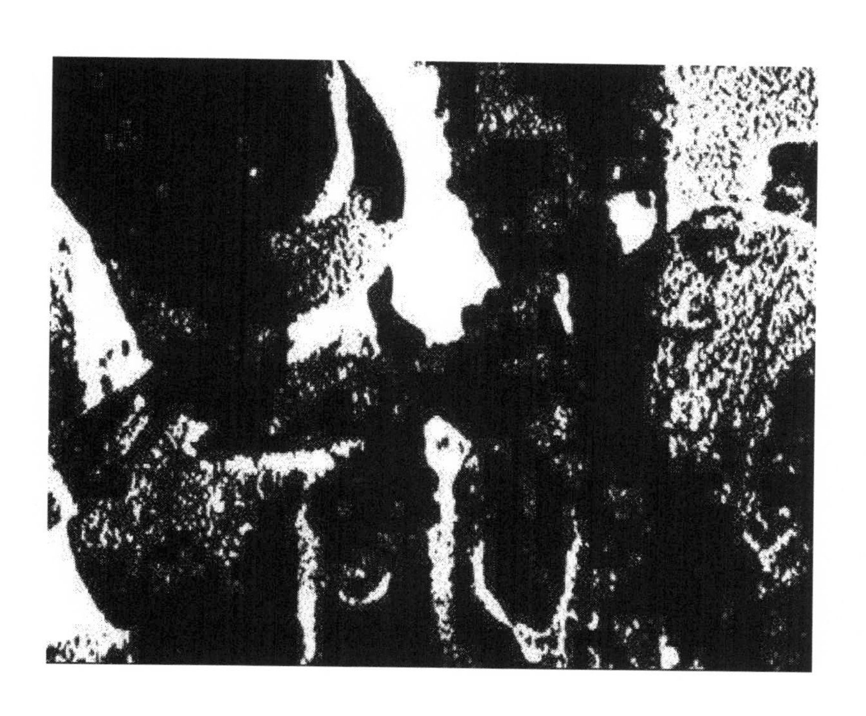

"*That's good. Good. Hold your position.*"

The voice comes to you amplified and slightly distorted. It's the voice of the woman, the leader, and it's obvious that she's using a bullhorn. Where the hell did she get a bullhorn? It's not a thought that occupies your mind for long, however, as the zombies continue to fill the street, to close in around you. The air is thick with the stench of them. You can smell them even over the less than appealing odor of the strips of dead flesh that decorate your body. To say that they stink would be a grand understatement. It is an odor that combines the sickly sweet smell of decaying flesh with that of various bodily excretions. The air is dead and still. What you wouldn't give for a little breeze about right now. The alcohol you had consumed with Grant–poor bastard–stirs within your stomach. You will yourself not to be sick. Not that you think any of those present would really notice.

"*OK, now walk around a bit. But not too far. A few steps one way. A few steps back. Stray too far and I'll give the signal to take you down. And remember, you're one of* them *now. So start acting like one of them.*"

When you finally rolled out of bed this morning could you have ever imagined that this is how your day would go? No, certainly not. If so, you more than likely would have stayed in bed.

"*Come on now. You better start making a show of it. I think some of them are getting suspicious.*"

It's hard to think about much of anything except trying to get away, just turning and running as quickly as you can. But you can't. For one thing, you believe the woman, that she will have you gunned down if you try something like that. And for another, chances are good that the zombies would react to such a display of un-zombie-like behavior. So, instead, you start to moan–that part comes easy what with the feeling in your stomach, the heavy sensation of dread filling your body, and the awful stench assailing you every time you take a breath–then you move, one slow limping step after another. Three steps forward. Turn to the right. Three more steps. Turn to the right again. Three more steps. And repeat. You make a rough square with your movements, being careful to avoid any contact with the walking dead all around you. The sound of your moaning is lost in the similar sounds coming from every imaginable direction. You are afraid. As afraid as you've ever been in your life. If any of the surrounding creatures gets wise to your act you know you're in serious trouble. If one of them attacks, you're certain that a feeding frenzy would follow. Hopefully the crazy woman who forced you out here would have enough mercy in her heart, withered and black as it may be, to have you gunned down before you suffered too much.

As you turn again, repeating the square for a second time, a rather large and obese zombie brushes up against you, pulling a flap of dead skin from your arm. It takes every ounce of willpower you have to not break and run at that moment. Somehow, you manage not to give in to the nearly overwhelming impulse. None of the undead seems to take notice of what has happened. As you will your racing heart to slow, you watch as a woman—or what used to be a woman—walking nearby shakes her arm rapidly a few times. The hand at the end of that arm, which seems to be hanging from nothing more than a single tendon, tears free and drops to the ground. It is accidentally kicked by the zombie walking behind her, disappears among the myriad shambling, shuffling feet.

Three steps, turn... Three steps, turn... Then the screaming starts. An awful, mad screaming that causes the fear stirring around inside you to rise up and wash down over you like a bucket of frigid water dumped over your head. The woman with the bullhorn must have some insight into what you're feeling as she gives you the following bit of advice:

"*I'm just letting you know once again: Try to run and we'll take you down. You've done well so far. But the real test is coming up. For your sake, I think you need to give this little role of yours everything you've got. Imagine what it's like to be one of these pathetic creatures. You used to be alive. Alive! And now you're not. Now you're a rotting, hungry thing with nothing on your mind but the next time you can get a taste of some living flesh. Now how does that make you feel?*"

She's treating you like you're some method actor on the set of a low budget horror movie. Who the hell does she think she is, George freakin' Romero? There's no doubt, as far as you're concerned, that the woman is certifiably nuts. And what does that make you? You're the one out here mingling with a mob of zombies and trying to pass yourself off as one of them. Not that you really have any choice in the matter...

The screaming gets louder. You continue walking, slowly, forcing a lack of coordination into your limbs. Three steps, turn. Three steps, turn. Like a malfunctioning robot waiting for someone to come along and reprogram it or shut it down. More screaming. Louder. Louder.

And then they are there.

Three of them. Howlers. You take a deep breath, nearly gag on it, force yourself to let it out slowly. *Keep walking... Keep walking... I am a zombie... They will not hurt me...*

The howlers stand in a rough triangle, watching you, surrounding you. The other, slower, full-fledged zombies make a point of walking around this makeshift triangle, like a river flowing around a large stone in its midst. You try not to make eye contact with any of the three screamers, to not even look at them, but it's next to impossible. In fact, you cannot look away. The madness in their stares, it draws you. The way they look at you, heads tilted to the side, on the verge of comprehension. Fairly mangled heads in two of the cases. One of them looks like it may have taken a bit of a curb stomping, the other like it lost a fight with some sort of wild animal.

They're onto me, you tell yourself. Any second now they're going to converge, do God knows what to you...

You have to get away. You have to make a break for it. Now. Right now!

"*That's it,*" comes the amplified voice. "*You're doing great. I think they're buying it.*"

The screamers look away from you. In the direction of the voice.

Yes, yes. Go to the voice.

One of them screams and heads over toward the doorway from which you emerged. It screams again and you see some of the slow zombies start to turn in that direction.

"*Oh, damn it.*"

There is the sound of a gunshot. For a moment you are convinced the shot is meant for you, that you'll feel the pain of the bullet's impact, that you'll be left for dead right there on the street. But there is no pain. There is more screaming, though. The other two howlers still standing nearby head in the direction from which the shot was fired. More gunfire. Groups of zombies turn in that direction.

This is your chance!

You force yourself to continue moving in the manner that you have been moving. Only this time, after three steps, you do not turn. You keep going. Northbound with the general flow of the undead mass surrounding you. With any luck, you'll be able to limp your way right on out of here.

Ten steps. Twenty. Fifty. You approach an intersection with a dormant traffic light. More zombies are approaching from the west. They blend with the crowd, half of which seems to be moving north, the other half toward the east. Gunfire erupts behind you. There is more screaming. You don't think all of it comes from the crazed zombies. You can only hope that the undead have been able to gain entrance into the building, that they've gotten their hands on the woman and her gun-toting crew. Maybe that's *her* screaming as the zombies bite and tear into her flesh. The thought makes you smile. It would be the least she deserves.

If you continue to the north, turn to page 196.

If you head east, turn to page 202.

She drives. South, then west. South, then west again. Directly into the heart of the matter, toward the genesis of all that has happened today. She drives into the stain.

A dark fog envelopes the vehicle, cutting off enough light to force the EMT to turn on the ambulance's headlights. It's fortunate that there's so little traffic in this part of the city. Everyone who could has long since fled. And those who had been turned, who became one of the hungry dead, went after them. At one point, however, a lone zombie stumbles in front of the ambulance. At least you hope it's a zombie. The driver does not slow the vehicle at all, just runs the shambling figure down. It's about then that Grant starts to howl from where he lies immobilized in the back of the vehicle. It is a painful, terrible sound. You don't think he can keep it going for long. But he does. He just goes on screaming like a man freshly condemned to the worst corner of hell.

Without warning, the EMT slams on the brakes. You reach out, brace yourself against the dash, see through the windshield what prompted such an immediate halt. A cement barricade standing as tall as the vehicle's hood blocks the road.

"End of the line," says the EMT. You can barely hear her due to the gas mask covering her face not to mention the din created by Grant's howling and thrashing against his restraints. The woman next to you makes a minor adjustment to her mask, spends a moment examining the DVR which is back in her hand. Then she kills the ambulance's engine, pulls the keys out of the ignition, and exits the vehicle without another word.

Moments later, the two of you are standing in front of the ambulance, looking over the barricade. You can't see very far in the mist surrounding you. The street is swallowed by darkness maybe twenty feet in front of you. Nothing moves in the limited area available to your perusal. Above, the sun is a dull, pale disk in the sky. Your breathing is loud within the confines of the mask. Each inhalation is a bit of a struggle. You assume that the mask's filters are working the way they should as you don't feel in anyway sick. Well, accept for the touch of anxiety you're experiencing at the thought of all that dark, deadly gas surrounding you.

"Let's go," you hear the EMT's muffled voice say and then, as you watch, she starts to pull herself up and over the concrete barrier. For a moment, you think about waiting in the ambulance. But Grant's in there. Or what used to be Grant. And you can hear him screaming from here. And seeing as how you're already here... Over the barricade it is.

On the other side, the two of you walk next to one another. The EMT has her camcorder out in front of her, view screen flipped open, panning the lens slowly back and forth. You pull your .38 free from where you've been keeping it stuck down the front of your pants, hold it out in front of you, finger on the trigger. No telling what might come rushing out of the mist without any warning at all.

The street you're following ends at a sidewalk with a patch of grass beyond. At the far side of this small yard area, the front wall of a building looms out of the mist. Or, at least what's left of the wall. There is a huge, ragged opening leading into the building, obviously the result of a very powerful explosion. The mist does seem a little thicker here although you'd have to assume that most, if not all, of the gas contained within the building has escaped by now. At least you hope this is the case.

"And here it is." You can hear the EMT providing narrative to what she is filming. "The source of all the misery that has befallen our city on this day. The place is curiously deserted. No doubt, the criminals responsible for–"

"Drop the camera," says the muffled voice of a man from behind you, "and the weapon. Now."

You feel the barrel of a gun press into the small of your back.

"You can't stop us from–" the EMT protests.

"Now!"

You drop the .38.

When the EMT goes to say something else, you look toward her just in time to see the butt of what appears to be a military issue machine gun come up and crack her across the side of the head. With a grunt, the woman drops the camera to the ground then falls to her knees.

Hands frisk you quickly, efficiently.

"Move!" says a different voice and the gun is pushed harder into your back.

You move.

Following instructions from your captors, you turn right and walk a short ways to a pair of glass doors that leads into the building the EMT had only moments earlier been filming. A flashlight comes on from behind you and you are told to walk through the lobby, enter the carpeted hallway beyond.

"Second door on the right. Go inside."

Through the doorway is an office. A trio of battery powered lights placed about the room make it easy to see the pair of figures seated on either side of the desk before you. The mist is thin in here, barely noticeable, but the room's occupants aren't taking any chances and are wearing gas masks of their own.

"What do we have here?" asks the person, a man, seated at the far side of the desk. He is dressed in military fatigues as is the more diminutive figure at the desk's near side.

"Found them outside snooping around," says one of the men, also dressed in full military garb, who brought you here. There are three of them, you can see now. One of them has the EMT's arm draped across his shoulders, a hand around her waist, keeping her on her feet. Her head lolls from side to side and you can hear her moaning incoherently. "They were armed. One of them had a camera."

The smaller figure seated at the desk says in a woman's voice without even looking your way: "No witnesses."

Icy fingers make a fist in your gut. You don't like the sound of that.

"Now wait a minute," you say.

"Quiet." The barrel of the gun is jammed painfully into your back.

"You heard her," says the seated man. "No witnesses."

"Yes, sir," says the voice of the soldier behind you. Then: "Let's go."

You are told to head further down the hallway, to enter one of the other offices there. All the while you're thinking you have to do something, *anything*. You have to make a break while you can. But it all seems surreal, like this really can't be happening. Events take on the quality of a dream. Your body doesn't seem to be your own as you obediently do as you're told. All the while you tell yourself that there's not a damned thing you can do anyway. There is a certain sense of inevitability to it all. Dropping to your knees on the office floor. Watching as the EMT is made to kneel beside you. The sound of the gunshot which throws the woman next to you forward, sprawling across the thin carpet. And then...

THE END

North. All the way to the goddamn North Pole if you're lucky. Anywhere but here. You walk. Breathing deeply, slowly all the way. Your hands are trembling. Adrenaline flows through your body like an electric current. How long and how far you walk you are not sure. It's like moving in a nightmare, like you're not really moving at all. Zombies shamble and moan all around you. Howlers run by, screaming in that maddening, terrible way they have. The dead flesh itches where it is stuck to your skin, the blood drying, scabbing. You can't help it, you scratch at it in places along your arms. The smell of the dead envelopes you. There is no wind here, not the slightest trace of a breeze. It is hot. The odor is thick and cloying. Like a walking slaughter house. It's like you're in Hell, a living Hell, condemned to walk like this among the dead for all eternity, on and on, forever and ever, until the end of time.

Screaming erupts from various places, near and far. Regular, human screaming. Sounds of terror and dismay. Half-eaten bodies lie in the street. To your right a trio of zombies drag a woman kicking and shouting out of the doorway of an apartment building, pull her down to the ground and have at her with hands and teeth. Along the way–to where, exactly, you're not sure, out of here hopefully, just out of here–you see others unfortunate enough to get caught up within the meandering crowd of the undead suffering similar fates. And, oh, how they do suffer. The looks of horror on their faces... The way their shouts rise in pitch and volume until it sounds as though their throats must rupture from the strain... And then the silence as those throats are torn out or some other vital, life sustaining pieces of their bodies are torn away and devoured.

Not much farther, you tell yourself, over and over again, a mantra to keep your feet moving and your head about you, not sure if it's even remotely true or not. *Not much farther now...*

You limp. You moan. You stay in character, hoping all the while that the monsters around you never wise up to your little charade. So far, they seem convinced by your previously untested acting skills. Or is it simply the dead flesh that adorns your body? A combination of both, more than likely. Best not to break character and test it either way. Keep on limping. Keep on moaning...

The minutes stretch on and on. Any time a zombie happens to glance your way you're convinced that the game is over, that your disguise has been penetrated, that it's about to be time for you to do a little screaming of your own. But it doesn't happen. The nightmare continues. The slow, interminable hell of it all.

And then...

Thwup-thwup-thwup-thwup...

Looking upward, you see it there, a great black insect hovering in the air above you. It is sleek and black with short, stunted wings, a long tail and a whirling appendage jutting from the top of its head which keeps it aloft. It can't be more than fifty feet above you, barely higher than the tops of the buildings to either side of the street you and your undead traveling companions have been following. One side of the flying beast is open and there is a man leaning out and looking down. Raising your hand, you wave at the guy. He's dressed in a blue jumpsuit, a helmet on his head, a dark visor down over his eyes. The man leans back into the helicopter for a moment, leans back out again. And again, you wave. This time the guy waves back. An amplified voice descends upon you from the hovering craft:

"*You there. Are you alive?*"

You cup your hands around your mouth, shout back: "Yes! Yes! I'm alive! Help me! Please!"

The voice again: "*Why aren't they attacking you?*"

Without even realizing it, you've stopped moving. A zombie bumps into you from behind, moans in your direction as it passes by.

"They think I'm one of them!" you answer. "Please, get me out of here!"

The man leans back into the helicopter. Another zombie bumps into you. Screaming reaches you from somewhere ahead. There is gunfire in the distance. *Pop! Pop! Pop!* Something is tugging at your sleeve.

Looking away from the helicopter and your chance of salvation, you see a particularly mutilated corpse standing next to you, one of the few remaining fingers on its right hand hooked under the end of your sleeve. In disgust and annoyance you slap the hand away then give the zombie a shove. It staggers backward into a few other passing zombies. You can't be bothered with this. The helicopter...

You look back up just in time to see the man leaning back out of the open doorway on the side of the craft. "Here you go then!" he shouts.

He drops a length of rope down toward you. It uncoils, the end of it hanging only a few steps before you at about eye level.

Yes!

"Put your foot in the end!"

You see that a loop has been fashioned there. But it's too high. You shout for them to lower the helicopter, just a bit. And, miraculously, they do. As you put your foot in the loop you feel that tugging at your sleeve again. And now on the back of your shirt. And as you watch, another zombie has turned around and is coming straight back toward you.

The gig is up, it seems.

"*All set?*" the amplified voice emanates from the helicopter.

"Yes! All set!" Your voice is tinged with hysteria. Something takes a more forceful grip on your arm. A hand comes down on your shoulder. And the one that turned around, it's practically in your face now. So it wasn't just the dead flesh, you tell yourself. The act was part of it too. Damn things are smarter than they look. Not much, certainly. But smarter all the same.

You take a tight grip on the rope just as the helicopter starts to rise. The hand on your shoulder falls away. As does the finger at your sleeve. Literally, it just tears away and falls to the ground. And the zombie that turned around... It lurches toward you, its face now waist high as you rise, then on a level with your knee. It reaches for your leg. With the foot that is not hampered by the loop at the end of the rope, you launch a kick at the creature. The toe of your shoe connects with the face of the dead thing with a satisfying *crunch!* But, quite miraculously, the thing manages to latch onto your pants leg with its hands. And, even more astonishingly, it manages to get its teeth into you, right in the unprotected space between the cuff of your pants and the top of your shoe. The sock you're wearing does nothing to stop the teeth from burying into the flesh of your ankles, causing a scream to erupt from your mouth. And now you're kicking and thrashing with a vengeance, trying desperately to dislodge the monster. Which, eventually, you do after you've risen about fifteen feet into the air. The zombie falls to the pavement, lands awkwardly and goes down, one of its legs sticking out at an odd angle. You take little joy from this victory, however, as the knowledge that you've been bitten by a zombie races through your mind. Bitten by a zombie! Are they infectious?! In the movies they're always infectious!

"Hold on tight!" comes a voice from above you. "Don't let go of the rope!"

You feel sick, tell yourself that it's all in your head, that you're not really physically ill. That even if they are infectious, the disease wouldn't have taken hold that quickly. Or so you try to convince yourself as you rise higher and higher into the sky, as the helicopter takes you north, away from the madness and the mayhem taking place on the ground below. Toward the river that borders the northern edge of the city you fly, not so far, no, not so far at all. Another ten minutes walking and you would have been there. But the barricade... You see it below. Uniformed soldiers behind portable, concrete walls firing indiscriminately toward the crowd before them. A crowd that you would have been a part of. But, instead, you're flying above it all, rescued, taken to safety by the blindest of luck. What are the odds? You may just be the luckiest person in the world. Or the city, at least. Except for that whole getting-bitten-by-a-zombie thing, of course.

Your ankle is throbbing. You're afraid to even look at it. *How much time do I have?* you wonder. How long before the change begins?

Caught up in these grim musings, the terror that you would normally experience at being whisked a hundred feet above the ground, dangling by a rope beneath a helicopter is somewhat muted. You are only afraid. Very afraid, yes, but not mind-numbingly so. Apparently, the people in the helicopter have no intention of reeling you in. Wherever you are headed, you're going to get there by dangling like a fish on the end of a line. The wind is tugging at your clothes. It is not a strong enough force to detach you from the rope, though, which you are clenching with white-knuckled hands.

And there's the river, directly below you now, it's dark waters undulating as they flow by to the east. For some reason, you feel a bit safer for the moment even though, realistically, a fall from this height and at this speed would probably kill you no matter the surface you land upon.

And then you're across the river and the helicopter is slowing its speed. The ground starts to come up, at a startling rate at first and then much more slowly as you hover a mere fifteen feet above the ground.

Ten.

Five.

Touchdown.

You pull your foot free of the loop. The amplified voice from above says, "*All right down there?*"

Raising your hand, you give a thumbs up. Then you're cupping your mouth again and shouting, "Thank you! Thank you so much!'

"*Just doing our job.*"

With that, the rope is pulled in and then the copter is rising, turning, heading back across the river on some other mission.

Turn to page 206.

East it is. Toward the bulk of the military presence. If you cannot find hope of rescue there, then where can you?

The journey is slow and it is many blocks to where the newscasters reported the military perimeter had been set up. You limp along, do your best imitation of the undead making the journey with you. Where they are heading, why they are heading anywhere, exactly, you have no idea. Surely, they are not moving in this direction for the same reasons that you are. You would assume that they have no idea what's waiting for them. And if they did, they would be making every effort to avoid it. Undoubtedly, they are just wandering, covering new ground, searching for new prey, for more humans to feast upon, to possibly swell their numbers. At least, that's what you think. But do you really know what goes on in the mind of a zombie?

Ahead, you hear raised voices, shouts, a few terrified screams. Not at all like the screaming of the howlers. No, these are live, human sounding screams. It would seem that the zombie horde has chanced upon a new food supply after all.

A couple more blocks and you reach the sight of the disturbance. It is a traffic jam. Cars are backed up on either side of the road, all pointed in the same direction, toward the east. For some reason, the flow of cars out of the city has been hampered here. Some sort of accident? A military blockade ahead? Both explanations make as much sense as any other. Although you have to wonder why the authorities would prevent all these people from leaving the city. Has the city been sealed off? Has it reached the point where nothing is permitted to leave, not just the walking dead? If so, coming this way may not have been such a wonderful idea after all. Not that the thought of turning around appeals to you all that much. That would involve going against the flow of the zombie traffic, drawing attention to yourself. Even if you are pretty sure that most of the undead would fail to notice any odd behavior on your part. The disguise seems to have effectively fooled them. You could probably find a sheet of cardboard and put on a break dancing demonstration and still draw little attention to yourself. These creatures really are not very bright. But there are the others. The howlers. The very thought of them causes your fingers to twitch nervously. No, you don't want to be noticed by those monsters. Best to keep your head down, keep limping, and just go with the flow.

The zombies are crowding the cars here, banging on roofs and hoods and windows with their fists. You hear the sound of glass crunching then glance to your left just in time to see a young woman pulled out of a car through the broken window. She screams and pleads for someone to help her. And you want to, you really do, but trying to play the hero would be beyond foolish. You aren't even armed. What could you really do? You look away as the biting and the real screaming begins and just keep moving forward.

The young woman is not the only one to suffer such a horrible fate along this stretch of road. Far from it. A locked car can only offer protection for so long against such a mindless and instinctively driven horde. Some people try to make a break for it on foot. A few even look like they have a chance of getting away. One fleeing individual bumps into you in his haste. You make a feigned grab at him, moan a little louder as he hurries past you. As long as you're doing this whole fake zombie routine you might as well take it as far as you can.

And then, seemingly out of nowhere, come the helicopters. They appear from over the roofs of buildings to either side of the road, swoop down like giant birds of prey that have spied a particularly tasting looking animal scurrying across the ground. And then they unleash hell with the machine guns and missile launchers that they carry.

Explosions shake the ground and a group of nearby zombies is shredded by the large caliber bullets a nearby hovering chopper dispenses. The sleek, black, flying military craft fire indiscriminately down toward the street, obviously unconcerned with any harm they inflict on anyone unfortunate to actually be alive in all this mess. And that would include you. More explosions shake the ground. Bullets chew up car roofs and asphalt and the fronts of buildings. Oh, yeah, and zombies too. Zombies by the bushel full. Realizing that the time for play acting has come to an end, you break into a sprint over toward the small flight of cement stairs that leads to the entrance of an antique shop. The place has a wooden door with a

"Closed" sign hanging from its handle. Hoping that the door can be pulled open, you reach for the handle... and find out just how much hoping will get you in times like these. Not much. In fact, right about now it gets you nothing at all. The door is locked. Turning around, you see that the road is thick with the dying and the dead, walking or otherwise. In the air above you there hovers a half dozen state of the art killing machines. One of which has just launched a missile toward where you are standing. It misses you, striking the cement staircase you have only just ascended instead. And that old saying, the one about close only counting as far as horseshoes and hand grenades are concerned... It seems that air-to-surface missiles count too. The force unleashed by the missile's detonation slams you into the front wall of the antique shop. It also pulls loose a couple of very important parts of your body, namely your left arm and the lower half of your right leg. You don't notice this, however, as the force of the impact has done some pretty terrible things to the back of you skull. A sudden and inescapable darkness obliterates the world.

THE END

You're standing in the parking lot of a strip mall with a road running past it a short distance away. There's a grocery store, an appliance store, a deli and a bakery. And there are military vehicles parked nearby. Jeeps. Large vehicles with white stars on the sides. A couple of tanks. There are fire trucks too. An ambulance. Another helicopter. A white, boxy truck with a red cross painted on the door.

A woman in a white uniform is approaching you as are two armed men in soldiers' garb.

You limp toward them, the bite on your ankle making its presence known every time you put weight on it.

"My ankle," you say.

Then the woman is walking beside you, the soldiers behind you. She asks your name. Blood type. History of allergies. You are led to the back of the truck with the red cross on it. A door is pulled open.

"Get in," says the woman. She offers you a smile. It does little to quell the feeling of dread seeping through your body.

"Am I going to..." You have to fight to get the words out. "Turn into... one of them?"

"Not if I can help it," she says.

There is a wide array of gear hanging on the walls of the truck. Air tanks. Gas masks. Heavy coats. Various high tech-looking gadgetry with which you are unfamiliar. Different types of monitoring devices, you assume. A padded bench runs along one wall.

"Sit," says the woman.

You comply.

She kneels down and opens a white, plastic box with a red cross on it that looks remarkably like a fishing tackle box. Reaching in, she removes a small glass vial of some clear liquid and a syringe wrapped in plastic. The sight of the needle makes you nervous.

"What's that for?"

"It will help with the bite. Any diseases associated with it."

Again you ask: "Am I going to turn into one of them?"

And again, she tells you: "Not if I can help it. Now roll up your sleeve." As she leans in close to you, she brushes at the dead flesh on your arm. "Very clever." She finds a vein at the inside of your elbow, sticks the needle into it. You hiss. With her thumb she pushes the clear liquid into your arm then removes the needle.

She stands before you, ducking a bit due to the low ceiling, staring down at you. "Try to relax."

You force a laugh. "Yeah, easy for you to say."

"Take a deep breath. That's it. Exhale. Another one."

Amazingly, you *do* start to relax.

"How do you feel?"

You shrug. "A little better, I guess."

She just stands there, looking at you.

"And now?"

"Better." You smile. "Yes, definitely better."

Another pause. "And now?"

"Hey. What was in that–"

And everything goes dark...

You awake in a well-lit white room. There are no windows. Two doors, one with a handle on it, one without. A twin-sized bed with clean white sheets upon which you lay. A small table next to the bed. You are not wearing the clothes you had on when...

It takes you a few moments to remember.

When you escaped the city. When the woman in the white outfit stuck the needle in your arm. Now you are dressed in loose fitting, white cotton pants. A white T-shirt. No shoes or socks. The air is warm but not too warm. Comfortable. Someone cleaned you up, disposed of the dead skin, washed your hair while you were out. Wrapped your ankle.

You get up, limp across the short distance to the door with the handle, open it. Bathroom. You have no idea where the door with the missing handle leads. Wanting to find out, you walk over to it, curl your hand into a fist and start to beat on it.

"Hey!" you shout. "Somebody! Anybody! What the hell is this?!"

You tire of this quickly, though. Whatever was in that needle still seems to be floating through your system. You return to the bed, sit on its edge.

Now what?

Your stomach gurgles. When was the last time you ate? You have no way of knowing since you have no idea how long you were out. What you wouldn't give for a chicken sandwich. At least there's a bright side: you're not craving human flesh.

Without warning, the door you were pounding on swings open. Two men step into the room. One of them is dressed like a doctor. White jacket. Stethoscope around his neck. He's middle aged. Wears glasses. Dark hair going grey near the temples. Very distinguished looking. The other man wears military gear. Helmet. Fatigues. A pistol in his right hand.

The doctor has a chart in his hands which he is looking at while nodding his head. He steps up before you, lowers the chart, raises his eyes, puts on his best professional smile.

"And how are you feeling?" he asks like he's continuing a sentence you never heard him begin.

"What the hell is going on here?"

The smile slips just a little.

"How are you feeling?"

The soldier takes a step forward. You get the picture."Fine. A little tired."

"Hmmm. Yes. To be expected. No strange... urges?"

You almost laugh. "No stranger than usual."

"Good. Good." He raises the chart again. "Everything here looks... normal enough. Considering."

"Where am I?" you ask.

"Close to home. Close to home. Well, what's left of it, that is."

There is a sinking feeling in your gut. "What does that mean?

"I'm afraid they had to bomb the place. Nuke it, actually. It was the only way. Things had gotten so far out of hand. Desperate times and all that..."

Your mind is reeling. It's too much to think about.

"And when will I get to leave here?"

The smile returns to its former glory. "We'll need to run some more tests, of course. Make sure that little bite you suffered doesn't have any unforeseen side effects. Although, I'm not anticipating any. It seems that the virus is of the strictly airborne variety, can only be contracted by inhaling it."

"How long?"

"A few weeks, I'd say."

"A few weeks?!"

"A couple of months, tops."

He turns his back on you, heads toward the door. "Don't feel bad," he tosses back over his shoulder. "You're one of the lucky ones, really."

He leaves the room. The soldier follows. The door closes.

And, yes, you are lucky. You survived the zombie outbreak. Got out before the nuclear strike. Nothing to do now except lie back and relax. Might as well get comfortable as it looks like you're going to be here a while.

Congratulations.

You were able to find the One Way Out.

You escaped from Zombie City.

THE END

Artist Biography

Thomas A. Erb is an author and artist of dark images and even darker words. His short works have appeared in several anthologies: *Dark Things II, Fell Beasts, Relics & Remains, Cadence In Decay* and *Vampires Don't Sparkle*, and Shroud Magazine. His novella, "Tones of Home" was part of the Twisted Tales from the Torchlight Inn collection. He has also edited the zombie anthology, *Death, Be Not Proud* for Dark Quest Books. He is currently working feverishly on a period zombie novel and is excited to tackle that market next. He holds a Master's degree in art education, and has designed several book covers. He helps pay the bills by providing freelance illustration and painting movable murals for the private and public sectors. He lives in upstate New York with his wife, Michelle and their two obnoxious dogs, Rask and Duchess, and dreams of someday moving to a place where he doesn't have to live through a snowpocalypse every winter.

You can learn more about Thomas's writing and artwork on Facebook and at his website: http://taerb.blogspot.com.

Author Biography

Ray Wallace hails from a suburb of Tampa, FL. His debut novel, *The Nameless* was published by Black Death Books in the winter of 2009. He has published more than twenty stories in such magazines and anthologies as *The Zombie Feed: Vol. 1, The Blackest Death Vol. 1 & 2, Chimeraworld 4* and *Erotic Fantasy: Tales of the Paranormal*. A few of his other stories have appeared on The Chiaroscuro website where he took first place in their second annual fiction contest. He also wrote a long running book review column for The Twilight Showcase webzine and now writes reviews for Chizine. He can be visited online at: raywallacefiction.com.

Curtis, a young college student is dragged to his first gay club by his best friend Jimmy for a night of dancing, drinking and sex...at least until the dead start to rise and attack the club. Trapped inside the Asylum are a small band of survivors, including a drag queen, a male stripper, a Vietnam vet bartender, a pretentious gay couple, and an unstable DJ. Will this motley crew survive the hungry undead rattling the sealed-off doors? Will they survive each other? Will they survive their own personal demons? Asylum recalls George Romero's classic Night of the Living Dead–except with more gore and a more current social message.

Trade Paperback
$9.95

82 pages
ISBN-13: 978-0984553563

"...an extremely fun, fast-paced read. Highly recommended for zombie fans, especially those purists who enjoy the classic Romero-inspired zombies."–Skull Salad Reviews, T.J. McIntyre

"...the story is handled from inside each of the characters in turn as they hole up against the zombie attack. Mark does a great job constructing unique back stories and traits for each character, which is a big plus. We're privy to their demons as death stares them in the face and there is a lot of emotional weight that adds depth to their predicament. I'm picky with story endings, but for me, Mark hit just the right notes in the final paragraphs—creating both a whimper and a resonant bang."–The Crow's Caw

What do you get when you cross Buffy the Vampire Slayer with equal parts Shaun of the Dead? Well... we're not sure, but Paul Jessup's Dead Stay Dead does an admirable job of trying!

Natasha is a ghost whisperer. Her roommate is a gypsy able to explode heads Scanners style with her mind. And campus has been overrun by zombies. What's a girl to do?

In Jessup's fast-paced, gore-packed novella you'll follow Natasha as she attempts to save her school (and humanity, she supposes) from an impending apocalypse. Funny, bizarre, and even a bit sad, fans of hardcore zombie fiction will find plenty to enjoy in Dead Stay Dead.

Trade Paperback
$9.95

82 pages
ISBN-13: 978-0984553594

"A fresh take on a popular genre. Paul Jessup has just the right blend of gore and giggles to keep you turning the pages." –Sean Cummings, author of SHADE FRIGHT, FUNERAL PARLOR & UNSEEN WORLD

"*DEAD STAY DEAD drops you off in the middle of a zombie apocalypse on a college campus. It's a world you may not escape without becoming one of them. It's comical homage to b-movie writing that is eerily smooth and fine tuned. The writing is rhythmic, descriptive, and can stand up in any genre."*—Amazon Review

Former Stoker Award-nominated editor Jason Sizemore compiles seventeen tasty, brainy morsels of zombie short fiction in The Zombie Feed: Volume 1.

Trade Paperback
$15.95

264 pages
ISBN-13: 978-0982159644

Zombie fiction from many sub-genres are represented here: zombie apocalypse, zombie survival, zombies in human society, zombie hunters, and more. And the one thread interlocking these disparate groups--ZOMBIE MAYHEM! This action packed anthology takes a syringe full of contaminated adrenaline-laced undead and slams 1000 CCs directly into your chest cavity.

Fast paced, yet thoughtful, The Zombie Feed: Volume I will sate your appetite... at least temporarily.

Cold Comfort by Nathaniel Tapley
This Final December Day by Lee Thompson
What's Next? by Elaine Blose
Rabid Raccoons by Kristin Dearborn
The Twenty-Three Second Anomaly by Ray Wallace
Not Dead by BJ Burrow
Tomorrow's Precious Lambs by Monica Valentinelli
The Fare by Lucien Soulban
A Shepherd of the Valley by Maggie Slater
Broken Bough by Daniel I. Russell
The Last Generation by Joe Nazare
Goddamn Electric by K. Allen Wood
Hipsters in Love by Danger Slater
The Sickness unto Death by Brandon Alspaugh
Lifeboat by Simon McCaffrey
Zombies on the Moon by Andrew Clark Porter
Bitten by Eugene Johnson

Made in the USA
San Bernardino, CA
10 February 2013